C000165829

GLASS
MEMORY

BOOKS BY MOUD ADEL

EARTH GUARDIANS SERIES

First Contact (prequel)

Invasion

Redemption

Resurrection

.

Wing of Light

Wing of Blood

Wing of Metal

• • •

ILLICITUM SERIES

Twelve Jackals

Glass Memory

Next in the series

Ascension Trials

www.moudadel.com

ILLICITUM
GLASS MEMORY

MOUD ADEL

MASTOPERIA
BOOKS

MASTOPERIA BOOKS
Tours - France

First published in 2019 under the name The Last Seed

New edition published in 2021

Second edition

Edited by Killling it Write

Proofed by Fantasy Proofs

Cover by Christina P. Myrvold

Map by Ilcorvo Artworks

ISBN 978-2-492762-06-2 (Hardback)

To be kept up to date about the author and his books, please visit
www.moudadel.com/newsletter
and sign up for the author's newsletter

To my parents

For doing their best and more to support me in my darkest days despite being a continent away.

I love you. I always have, and always will.

LAND OF THE FUTURE

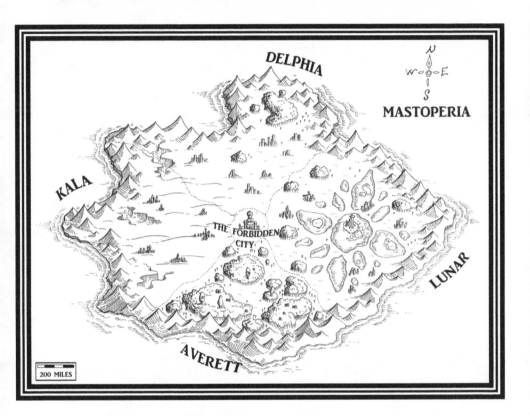

DELPHIA

MASTOPERIA

KALA

THE FORBIDDEN CITY

LUNAR

AVERETT

200 MILES

ALITA VARN

131 - Unknown

Land of the Future is the 8th piece of artist Alita Varn's secret collection - found after her mysterious disappearance in 169. The map depicts the continent of Mastoperia 800 years in the future. In 942, the cartography division at the university of Delphia confirmed that the map matches our present world with 89% accuracy.

PROLOGUE

250 Years Ago

Nothing remains unchanged, not even a dead desert, for all it takes is a little wind to carry a grain of sand from one place to another, and the surface of the planet is forever changed. It may not be visible to the naked eye, but one grain atop another can build hills and carve valleys. However, some don't make it to their destination, like the few specks Aira crushed with her feet as she walked through the desert, her white sneakers leaving marks that would soon disappear.

Aira, of course, didn't think about any of that. Instead, she paid attention to the music coming out of the black box hanging over her shoulder by a strap that fell to her tiny waist. She moved her head with the fast rhythm, her arms and torso also dancing to the beat while her long golden hair flapped behind her back.

The sun had just started to rise, and all Aira could feel was the cold touch of the morning on her sandy-colored skin. When one song ended and another started, her steps abandoned their regular pattern and started moving at a chaotic speed, matching that of the drummer's. She spun and turned, creating waves in the ground, dancing her way across the open desert, one song at a time.

When her playlist came to an end, she halted and turned her gaze to the sky. Seconds after, a lotus-shaped pod flew just above her, and she followed it with her eyes as it moved a little farther, then stopped midair before turning and flying back to her.

The pod came to a stop again above Aira and flew down until it was hovering less than two feet above the ground. Aira's grin widened as she saw the stranger sitting at the center of the pod, a twenty-something female with black hair and matching color eyes.

The stranger inspected Aira from top to bottom. "Yellow skin, wide white suit, and walking like the world is waiting on you. Let me guess, you are the Delphian candidate."

Aira smiled. "I would say the suit was enough to give away my origin, but sure, why not stereotype at the same time."

"I didn't mean—"

"Don't worry about it, Kalita. It's still nice to meet you."

Kalita drew her brows together. "You know my name? Of course, you know my name." She shook her head while exhaling. "What else can I expect from someone who sees the future?"

"A lot, but that's not what you're really after," Aira said, walking toward Kalita, presenting her hand for a shake. "Aira, the Delphian candidate as you expected."

Kalita looked at Aira's hand then met her eyes. "Why are you so nice? We are about to compete against one another to see who will become the Umholi and who will be an Illicitum."

"So?" Aira shook her shoulder, her open hand still opposite Kalita. "Regardless of who will become what, we are bound to live together for the next two and a half centuries. We need to be friends, don't you think?"

Kalita nodded and shook Aira's hand. "In this case, let me ask you, are you planning to walk all the way to the palace?"

"My legs are my only method of transportation."

"I see." Kalita stepped off her pod and touched its bottom before the flower-shaped device shrunk into a small yellow seed that fell into her palm. She grasped the seed with her two fingers and placed it at a predestined spot on the top of her right arm. "Now what?" she asked.

"Now, we walk until we run into Rhett, though this next encounter won't go as smooth as ours did." Aira started walking, Kalita by her side.

"Why not?"

"Rhett doesn't want to become an Illicitum. He is upset about leaving his family behind, but he can't abandon his duty."

"I'm assuming he is the Kalangou candidate then."

"You are correct again."

Kalita smiled, and Aira glanced at her through the corners of her eyes but said nothing as Kalita spoke again. "Do you always know everything that will happen?"

"It depends."

"On what?"

"On the fact that I won't be revealing that information to you until our little competition is complete."

"Then I guess the answer is no."

Aira turned to Kalita. "You are not an easy opponent."

"Neither are you, but now I'm wondering if the challenge started already."

"I thought it did the moment our factions declared us their candidates."

Narrowing her eyes, Kalita stopped and pushed Aira's arm, turning the latter toward her. "You knew I was coming, and you stopped, so I would come down and talk to you."

"Of course, I did. I thought we already established that."

"Maybe, but you didn't say that you did it to evaluate me."

"Kalita, don't pretend to be righteous. You took the long path around the palace, hoping to find one of us and measure our powers. It's why you came down to talk to me."

Kalita took a step forward, raising a finger at Aira and speaking with a charged voice. "Who are you to talk as if you know me?"

"For now, your equal. And put down your hand. There's nothing wrong with assessing one another, and I still want to be your friend like I said."

"You and I will never—"

At that moment, Rhett landed from the sky, leaving the plank of wood he stood on hanging midair. His arrival attracted the attention of both girls and interrupted Kalita. He was a large man with wide shoulders and a bald head. His onyx-colored skin glinted under the sun as he approached the other two.

"What seems to be the problem here?" Rhett asked.

Aira rolled her eyes. "Relax, Rhett, you are not an Illicitum yet. You don't need to act like one."

"What did you say, Delphian?" Rhett raised his voice, his chest jutting out and his veins popping.

"Don't pay attention to her. She is just trying to estimate your power through your behavior," Kalita said, taking her yellow seed off her right arm and throwing it in the air before the seed blossomed into a huge flower-shaped pod.

"I didn't ask you for your opinion, Lunardis," Rhett said, talking to Kalita. "I'm not afraid of a white-collar Delphian. I was on the council of my faction before becoming a candidate."

"Suit yourself," Kalita said, then jumped inside her pod and flew away.

When Kalita left, Rhett and Aira met each other's eyes. "Thank you," the latter said.

Rhett seemed to be confused by her words as he took a step back and scratched his head. "What for?" he asked, his voice calm.

"When you arrived, I was arguing with her, and you saved us before it escalated. I shouldn't have taken my frustration on you, though. It was wrong, and I'm sorry about that."

Rhett drew his brows together, his posture relaxing. "Don't worry about it," he said and waved his hand before the plank of wood flew down. "You need to learn to fight your own battles, though." Rhett stepped on the plank and waved his hand again, flying away in the same direction as Kalita.

Aira followed him with her eyes as he disappeared in the distance, her grin wide. When she was alone again, she continued walking. *Initial assessment, correct,* she thought. *Kalita is attentive to her surroundings and is often right about her observations. Her weakness is in believing that she is always right and how it riles her when someone points out her arrogance. Rhett is also strong, and he knows how powerful he is. He also possesses great knowledge about other factions and understands exactly how their powers work since he knew about our system of colored collars. However, he has a soft heart under his line of muscles and can be vulnerable to manipulation.*

"The next couple of centuries will be fun," Aira said out loud as she inverted her collar, revealing its true color of brown.

She put her music back on and continued toward the palace, her head moving with the beats, her body dancing to the rhythm.

THE ROOM IN WHITE

Present Day

"Most people are not lucky enough to work in a job they like. I am not most people. Yet sometimes the world forces us to walk away from the things we love for a chance at life."

"Miss Orantine, I didn't ask you to start your story yet."

"Is this not why I'm here?" *Please, don't make this investigation go longer than it needs. If I don't get out of here by the end of the day, I won't have enough time to save her.*

"Yes, but there are protocols that we have to follow. Please state your name, age, and faction of origin for the record."

Stupid questions that he already knows the answers to. But this is not the time to argue. "Orantine Maray, Thirty-nine. My faction of origin is Lunar."

"Is this the first time the Delphian intelligence investigates you?"

"You already know that it isn't." *I can't believe this.* "Can you please ask the important questions? I don't have time to waste."

"Miss Orantine, I have to follow the protocol. The polygraph must record all the answers before you tell your story. Otherwise, the recording won't be acceptable, and I won't be able to allow you to return to your faction as you wish."

Polygraph? Did he say polygraph? Where is it, though?

I can see the six cameras they tried to hide behind the wall. They should have known that a room wrapped entirely in white LED lights would easily reveal its secrets. There is a camera in each corner, one in the middle of the wall behind me and another inside the opposite wall, behind him. I can see the black spots they leave on the surface. Then there's this white rectangular-shaped table between him and me and our matching LED-lit chairs. But there's nothing else in this room, so where's that polygraph. And *since when do Delphians have top-of-the-line technology?* Technology is my faction's skill. They always relied on us to get modern gadgets, yet I doubt my people would give them such a machine that they could use against us.

"Miss Orantine, I need you to repeat your answer clearly, please."

Please! He sounds so polite. His features and pose portray the same too. Blue round eyes that are focused on me enough so that I believe I'm the center of his attention, though they dart to the stack of papers in front of him every now and then to avoid making me uncomfortable. His small lips are perfectly lined together, showing no signs of his demeanor, neither frowning nor smiling. Unwrinkled nose matching the sandy color of his skin. He must be in his early twenties. His arms are always on the table to make me feel safe and far enough from each other, so he appears inviting. This is a man who knows what he is doing. His clothes appear to be the standard outfit of Delphia, a white suit made of silk, loose enough so he can freely run in it. His collar appears to be different, though. It's green. I know they use the color of their collars to differentiate ranks, but I've never seen green before.

"Miss Orantine, are you still with me? I thought time was important for you."

Right! I need to stay away from my overthinking, at least for now. "This is the second time the Delphian intelligence interviews me. The first was seventeen years ago when I asked for permeant admission into Delphia."

"You are here today because you have asked to revoke that asylum and return to your faction. Is that correct?"

"Yes."

"Why do you want to leave Delphia?"

"Because I need to be in Lunar before tomorrow."

"I will repeat my question, Miss Orantine, and I would like a clear answer with an actual cause if you want us to move on. Why do you want to leave Delphia?"

"I don't feel comfortable telling you the answer." *I don't know what you would do with my words.*

"Then I won't be able to continue with this investigation, and I have no choice but to refuse your request."

Why are you standing and gathering your papers? No, wait! "Sit please, I will tell you."

"I will remind you that you can't lie. One lie will result in an immediate refusal."

"I'm aware." *Okay, let's not overthink this. I will just tell him, and it will be alright. Oh no, I need to blink back that tear. This is not the time to show vulnerability. Focus Oran, focus.*

"I received news that Lantrix is going after my daughter."

"Lantrix, the video game company?"

"Yes. My daughter used to work there, and they had some sort of fallout. It seems she discovered some information that they don't want the public to know, and they are now trying to silence her."

"Wouldn't that be a crime?"

"Not for a large, influential company like Lantrix. They have the politicians in their pocket."

"What do you think they will do?"

"Kill her." *Maybe even worse. They could strip her of her seeds, turning her into an empty shell.*

"How do you plan to prevent that?"

You're going too far with your questions. "Is this part of the investigation?"

"Your answers are what steers this investigation. Therefore, yes, it is part of the investigation."

I hate that Delphian power. It teaches them how to avoid any loophole. "As a spy, I still have connections in Lunar. I'm sure I can do something."

"Are you still a spy, Miss Orantine?"

"Former spy."

"When was the last time you had contact with Lunar?"

"Contacting my faction doesn't mean I was spying for them while living here."

"Fair enough. When was the last time you fulfilled any duties for Lunar?"

"Seventeen years ago, before I moved here."

"Alright, Miss Orantine—"

"Please call me Oran if you plan to call me by my name every two sentences."

"I can't do that, Miss Orantine."

Ugh... Delphians and their rules.

"I will start again, Miss Orantine, since you interrupted me the last time. All your answers appear authentic. Before we move on, I would like to remind you about the rules of this investigation."

Yes, please waste more of my time by telling me things I already know.

"This meeting will determine whether you can return to your faction or not. If you collect the needed points and I accept your exit request, you won't be able to return to Delphia, neither as a visitor nor as a resident. You can never request another admission, even from your own faction. If I refuse, you have the right to appeal. Once. If the appeal is also refused, you could renew your request in a year's time. Is that clear?"

"Yes." *Speak faster.*

"I would also like to remind you that if I refuse your request and you leave this faction regardless, it will be considered a hostile action, and we will be entitled to request a hunt from the Palace Illicitums who will rip off your six seeds. Is that clear?"

"Yes." *Should I think about what I would do if he refused my request? No, no, I can't focus on the negative now. I just need to make sure that my story is compelling enough for him to let me go, and everything will be okay. Will it be, though? One thing at a time, Oran. One thing at a time.*

Why is he grabbing his pen and reaching for the stack of paper in front of him? "What are you writing? I thought this was a recorded investigation."

"I just need you to sign these papers. They state everything we just said."

"Fine, where do you want me to sign?"

"On each paper, under my name."

"Breto Namara? Are you related to Dairo Namara?"

"Yes, did you know him well?"

"A little." *Let's not make a conversation out of this. I don't want to regret my question.* "Here. All signed." *And with a fake smile just for you.* "Shall we begin?"

"Yes. I heard your record from the last investigation, and I understand you asked for asylum after your superiors betrayed you. I would like you to tell me the story from the moment your life got complicated up to your arrival in the building today. Please be clear and precise with the events since I won't be asking questions during the time you tell me the story. The more information you give me, the easier it will be for me to make a clear decision that will hopefully be in your favor. Are we on the same page?"

"Yes."

"Please start then, and I will listen."

"It all began seventeen years ago when I received a call from my director asking me to meet him at headquarters. I knew from his tone of voice that something was wrong, which made me nervous. The director never worried about anything before that day.

"I still remember the echo of my red heels clapping against the marble floor when I walked into the building. My knees were stiff that day, not as flexible as usual. My calves tensed with each step. My stomach was flat, hiding the set of muscles I trained hard to gain. My shoulders stayed up, making me appear taller than I am, and my small breasts felt heavier than normal. I must have been paler than usual as well because while I walked through the hallway of the fourth floor where the meeting room was, three people asked me if I was sick."

"Excuse me, Miss Orantine, I know I said I wouldn't interrupt, but when I asked you for more details, I didn't mean a full-body description of how you felt. I just want the story in detail, not how everything looked."

"Of course." *Thank the lotus. I didn't want to keep going like that.*

PART ONE

Master Spy

EYE CONTACT

When I walked into the meeting room, I saw the director talking to three Delphians.

"Oran, you are finally here. Come, I will introduce you," the director said, his voice empty of its typical enthusiasm. "With me are Nir, Matso, and Ienta." He pointed at them one by one before he turned his head to them. "My dear friends, I would like you to meet Oran, one of my best officers."

The three answered with "nice to meet you" in a unified sound as if they trained on mastering the phrase together. Nodding in response, I sat next to my director, across the table from the others.

"What's wrong, boss?" I calmly asked, though my heart was racing, not knowing what to expect.

"Kala's council leader fought an entire tribe from Averett on his own, and it seems he won the fight."

"Rakamai?" I exclaimed. My eyes widened, and I noticed Ienta's brows draw together as she turned her face to me.

"Do you know him?" she asked.

"Not personally."

My boss rested his arms on the table as the corners of his lips slightly lifted. "She ran an investigative report on him two years ago."

I wondered how he could give the Delphians secret information that easily? I even squinted, looking at him, but his face remained focused on our guests.

Matso locked his eyes with mine, displaying a small smile that was barely visible. "What was your evaluation?" he asked.

I knew the moment I saw the corner of his lips lift that he used his faction's power of saiting to investigate the future and see my answer. I contemplated saying nothing just to mess with his power, but a nod from the director forced me to talk.

"Kalangous' power depends on the strength of the connection they have with their magical gates. No one outside Kala knows how the gates work or where they are exactly, but our researchers have discovered that this strength also affects their characters. In other words, we can measure how strong they are by observing their day-to-day behavior.

"Rakamai appeared calm on the surface but was known to be sensitive and highly emotional at times. All are characteristics of a weak link since the gates made them colder and dedicated in their missions." I looked at my boss, who followed what I was saying like the others as if he didn't know what I was talking about. "I gave Rakamai six out of ten. He didn't seem to be the strongest council leader."

Nir shook her head. "Clearly, your results were inaccurate."

"Possibly." I nodded. "But this was also two years ago. Kalangous are famous for having leaps in their power when they are in danger."

"Maybe—" Nir started, but I interrupted her as I could feel that whatever she was going to say would be insulting to my intelligence.

"The evaluation doesn't matter." I took my voice to a higher tone and added, "If he won the fight, then we need to take precautions. Serious ones. He obviously reached a level that we can no longer underestimate."

Matso looked at me with the same faint smile. It started to annoy me. "What do you propose we do?" he asked.

"Since I'm here, I assume we are planning an assassination."

"That won't be needed. Rakamai is dead."

"What?" My eyes widened. I looked to the director to ask him why he didn't tell me, but the expression on his face proved that he didn't know before this moment either.

Matso moved his gaze to the hand he kept on the table while displaying a smirk. "I can see you didn't get the full report, but Rakamai died at the end of the battle due to his wounds. At least, this is what the Illicitums want us to think."

"And you don't believe them?" I wanted to slap his mouth back into its correct position. Even though he was no longer facing me, I sensed he wasn't taking this meeting seriously or at least that he was hiding something.

"It doesn't matter what I believe. What I think, however, is that since Rakamai is dead, this meeting is pointless."

"I disagree." My voice was sharp, surprising me at first. "He may be dead, but that doesn't mean there aren't others who could have his level of strength. We need to reinvestigate everyone who is in a position of power. We can't wait until another Kalangou reaches Rakamai's level."

Matso turned back to me, his smile now filling his face. "Miss Oran—"

"That's Orantine to you." I met his eyes with a sharp stare, but he ignored me and continued.

"I understand you don't have the power to see the future like us, but by the time we return to our faction, we will learn that the Kalangous and Averettis fixed their feud internally. Their war is over, and it can no longer affect us."

"You're right. I don't have the power to see the future, but a quick look at the past is evidence enough that this won't be the last war. We can't stop taking precautions because we are currently at peace."

"Enough." The director placed his palms on the table as he stood. "I sat in silence and let you go at one another in case you could discover something we missed, but your argument serves no purpose."

"This is not—"

"I said enough, Oran." He turned his body toward me and slightly shook his head. "We will respect the peace between the factions."

I lowered my head in silence. Reading his body language, I realized he wanted to tell me that I couldn't discuss this further with the Delphians.

At that moment, the three Delphians left their seats and moved to the door, greeting the director and me on their way out. Matso was the last to shake my hand.

"I expect we will see each other again soon," he said so quietly that only I could hear. His arrogant smile remained stuck to his face. I narrowed my eyes, but before I could utter a word, he moved to the exit.

When only the director and I remained in the room, he looked at me with a wide grin on his face. "You did good, Oran. I'm proud of you."

"What?" I tilted my head, not knowing what to think. *What did he mean by I did good?* I wondered. When I shook my head and turned my gaze back to him, he was already at the door.

"I will expect you in my office in thirty minutes. You have a new mission."

He then opened the door and said over his shoulder, "And Oran, prepare yourself. This will be your hardest mission yet."

A NEW MISSION

I paced back and forth in front of the director's office, waiting for the thirty minutes to pass. The red seed on the left side of my chest blinked quickly while my heart raced. I wasn't sure how I felt about this turn of events, but I convinced myself I was excited. The moment the hologram of a watch around my wrist ticked the right time, I knocked and entered the director's office, even before he gave me permission.

He was behind his desk, going through a stack of papers, and appeared to be reading each piece carefully. When I approached the desk, he motioned for me to sit. I sat opposite him rocking my feet as I waited for him to speak.

"Relax. I will tell you everything." His eyes remained focused on the words he was reading.

"So? Will you send me to Kala to investigate the new council as I suggested?" The corners of my eyes lifted in question.

"No." He tidied his stack of papers and placed them in his office drawer before locking it with his thumbprint. "You will go to Delphia."

"To do what?" I raised my brows. "They are our allies."

"That doesn't mean we shouldn't keep an eye on them, right?" He smiled.

"But we never did before, and there's a good reason for it." I sighed. "They will see me coming. There's no way I could infiltrate their faction without them knowing about it."

"I chose you for this mission because you are the only one who can do it."

"Boss, you are not hearing me. No one can do it. They can see the future."

"Only their own future, not everything."

"Yes, but I'm bound to interact with at least one of them. They could see what I'm up to then. The Delphians are trained to see even what we don't want to say."

"I know." His grin widened. "Do you want this mission or not?"

"Why now? What changed?"

"I will tell you if you accept the job."

I took a deep breath and closed my eyes. The concept of doing what no Lunardis had done before tickled my brain, but it was also the first time I doubted myself. I wasn't sure I could do it. I asked the director to allow me a few minutes to think it over, then moved back into the hallway.

I paced in a circle contemplating what could happen if they caught me. The blue seed on the left side of my forehead blinked as I thought of the worst-case scenarios, but one idea kept pushing away all other thoughts. I had a chance to play the spy game with its true masters. Winning it would mark me as the best of the best.

I moved back to the director's office, unsure of what I was going to say, but my words made my decision for me. "I will take it," I said to my surprise as soon as I entered the office.

The director smiled. "I knew it. Now close the door. It's time to discuss the mission."

I sat in front of him as he pulled out a slim green file. "Our alliance with Delphia requires that we share files on our official personnel. We collect certain data on every person that will take a leadership position and send it to Delphia, and they do the same."

"That sounds weird. Why would we do that?"

"Transparency and insurance," he said quietly. "This allows us to build trust with one another, but also each faction would know how to retaliate and who would cause the biggest damage if either party tried to betray the other."

"How does this affect my mission? Are we retaliating for something?"

"Not yet." He shook his head. "Two days ago, we received a new record for their latest head of correspondence."

"That's good. It means the Delphians are still keeping their end of the deal."

"This is it." He handed me the green file. I opened the file to find only one piece of paper with handwritten information on the top.

Name: Matso
Age: Twenty-four

"There's basically nothing here."

"Exactly." He narrowed his eyes. "The smallest file we have on someone is one hundred filled pages."

"Do you think they are hiding something?"

"Either that or they don't know anything." He started to fidget with one of his gold pens on the desk. "Your mission is to know everything about Matso, and I mean *everything*."

I turned my gaze back to the file, reading the five words on its page repeatedly until I remembered the words Matso muttered to me on his way out.

"This mission will fail." I looked up at the director. "Matso told me that we would meet again on his way out. He clearly knows that I will go after him."

"Maybe," the director stated in a quiet voice. "I didn't say this mission would be easy."

"This is supposed to be a stealth mission. If the enemy knows already that I will investigate him, he has the advantage." I sighed. "I don't see how I can make this work."

"Did I overestimate your abilities?" He rested his back against his chair. "I thought you said you accept the mission. Are you having second thoughts?"

I stared at him in silence, my brain vacant of words.

"You know what?" He leaned forward. "Don't worry about it. We will erase this conversation from your memory, and I will find someone else to do it."

"No," I said, surprising myself for the second time. It was the last thing I wanted to say, but my tongue seemed to speak on its own. "I will do it. There's no one better than me."

"Alright then, the mission is yours, but you can no longer mention how hard this job will be. From this point forward, I want you to focus on solutions, not problems."

I raised my hand to my mouth before I said anything else. I didn't know what my brain wanted from me, and I feared letting it free.

The director tilted his head down for a few seconds before meeting my eyes once again. "I want to know your analysis of the situation."

I took a deep breath as my blue seed continued to blink in a random beat showing my scrambled thoughts. "You received the file two days ago, and Matso showed up today in our faction. It's possible the Delphians are plotting something."

"It could also be a coincidence. Their last correspondence director died in a battle against the Kalangous, and Matso's title allows him to be here. He has to be a witness."

"True, but they should have known his appearance along with his file, would arouse suspicion."

"Or they genuinely don't know."

I narrowed my eyes at him. "Are you on their side?"

"I'm just exploring all the possibilities."

I sat in silence for a few seconds, looking at the director. Acting as the opposing voice when brainstorming was a common technique used in Lunar, but something felt off this time. My intuition confused my boss's motives. I wasn't sure if he was genuinely trying to look at all possibilities with me or if he was trying to defend Delphia. I shook my head to get rid of my thoughts and return to the present before I stood.

"I will need time to think this through and find a viable plan."

"Four days. This is the time you have, and then your mission starts."

I nodded and moved toward the door. I didn't feel that four days were enough. Then again, I wasn't sure I could do it at all.

DEEP IN THE HEART

I decided to walk home that day and not use my lotus-shaped pod as usual. I wanted time to think, but I found myself focusing on the city instead.

Everything changes so quickly in Lunar that cities can become unrecognizable in the span of a few months. The glass billboards on the side of the road appeared ancient next to the new hologram ones. The walls were now an advertising space as well, with looped videos. Even the main road below the hovering pods was now a space to promote consumerism. I wondered about how our innovative faction shifted its focus to consumption instead. The sidewalk now had a moving part for those who didn't want to use their lotus pods but were too lazy to walk. People didn't pay attention to one another anymore. Everyone fidgeting with something or got lost inside their own heads where they projected media only they could see, ignoring the world around them.

They said it was a breakthrough when they found a way to broadcast videos directly to the purple seeds on the right side of our foreheads. I thought they would use it for education, but it seems the thought never even crossed their minds.

Lantrix and Ontar jumped on the service to monopolize it in a vicious war between two of our largest corporations. Ontar won that one and turned the technology into a streaming service with a monthly subscription to see all the movies you want from the comfort of your own head. I felt a pang in my stomach when I realized that the alternative was taking your purple seed off your body and placing it on a surface to turn it into a screen. I hated realizing how lazy we had become.

I looked at those who walked around me and saw how their figures had become thicker than I remember. It made me sad to see my beloved faction lose its soul as the pinnacle of our genius minds focused only on entertainment.

I couldn't take it anymore, so I grasped the yellow seed on my right arm and through it in the air before it blossomed into a rigid lotus. I took a step back, watching it grow larger and floating above the ground. When it reached full size, I sat in it and thought of my destination before my pod took me home.

My smile returned to me the moment I opened the door to my two-bedroom apartment. I smelled the rosemary and thyme infused with my favorite scent of a perfectly roasted chicken, but it wasn't the only reason I smiled. There was only one explanation for detecting my favorite food—he was back.

My grin widened as the music I only now noticed playing in the background became louder as I moved toward the kitchen. Resting a shoulder and the side of my head on the door frame, I watched him stir the soup.

For a second, I thought the world moved in slow motion. His silky blond hair flapped atop his tall figure as he moved his slim body to the music. I could've sworn that when his fingers released the salt into the soup, I saw every grain fall on its own. When I saw the corners of his brown eyes lift as he turned around to look at me, I wanted to run into his arms, but he was a man of precision who liked to take his time. Even though we had been married for four years, I still got a tingle in my stomach that had me wanting to appear cool in front of him. He was the only boyfriend I ever had, and we tied the knot when I turned eighteen. Everyone told me it was too soon, and we were both too young to know if we were absolutely right for each other, but we didn't care. We knew we were meant for one another.

"I thought you would be in my arms by now." He walked around the table that centered the kitchen.

I couldn't contain my legs any longer and ran toward him, jumping on his body. He knew me too well. I locked my arms and legs behind his back and cradled his upper lip with my tiny ones, gently pressing as our mouths unified in infinity. When I heard the soup timer go off, I grunted, believing that he would put me down, but he didn't. He carried me to the stove and freed only one arm to turn it off before pressing his lips against mine, again and again, allowing me to taste their sweetness.

"Let's move to the bedroom," I whispered in his ear.

"Not yet." He put me down, then looked at my frown and planted a quick kiss on my lips. "First, we eat. Second, we check on Evailen, and then..." He winked.

"How is she?" I asked.

"Sound asleep." He brushed his hand against my cheek. "Go check on her, and I will prepare the table."

I nodded and moved to her room. When I married Bodya, I believed I had a perfect life, and nothing could make me happier, but Evailen proved me wrong. The moment I felt her first kick in my womb, I knew that I was moving up a level in heaven. No, more like ten levels. This is how it felt to hold her. She was the last missing element in the equation of perfection.

I stared at the decoration on her walls, filled with her favorite movie and game characters and wondered if there was a space to add new ones. When she asked for a new character for her third birthday a month before, we had to repaint an entire wall to squeeze it in. I couldn't say no. It was the first time she could request something for her birthday.

I sat on my knees next to her small bed and couldn't help but spend long moments gazing at her features. I brushed her hair away from her face. It was black like mine, though soft like her father's. I wished she would awaken so I could see her blue eyes. I liked to get lost in them.

33

Bodya always said we had the same color eyes, but I disagreed. Her blue is sky-like, a reminder of the endless universe, while mine resembles the depth of a lake where everything drowns.

I looked down at her face with a small smile. Her seeds glowed brighter than I had ever seen, and I couldn't wait for her to be old enough so I could teach her how to use each of her six seeds. They're what gives us our power and the advantage to be superior in this world.

"Dinner is ready."

I heard Bodya's voice come softly through the doorway as he spoke in barely more than a whisper so as not to wake her. After kissing Evailen's head, I joined him by the door before he took my hand and held it for our ten-second stroll to the table in the kitchen. The plates were aligned beautifully with a candle centering the soup and the chicken in the middle of the table.

"It smells delicious," I said as he pulled out a chair for me.

I shook my head and pretended to frown, but he said nothing, only smiling as he moved to his seat. I would never tell him, but I secretly loved how he chose to stick with long-dead traditions. He waited for me to fill my bowl before he took hold of the soup's spoon to fill his own.

"I thought you wouldn't be home for another two days," I said as I put the spoon in my mouth, feeling every single taste bud lust for more.

"We finished the project earlier than anticipated."

The corners of my mouth lifted. "So, will you tell me what you invented this time?"

"We agreed not to talk about our work, didn't we?"

"Only when it's secret."

He put another spoonful of soup in his mouth, saying nothing. We worked at the same agency together, though in different departments. I was a field agent while Bodya worked in inventions and innovations. His team worked on various projects, but he only ever told me about the gadgets they created for field usage.

"That sucks." I put my bowl aside and grabbed my plate to fill it with chicken and potatoes. "I wanted to talk to you about the mission I received today."

"Is it secret?"

"Top." I chuckled.

"After the meal then." His expression turned serious. I could see he didn't want to talk about work, but I believed he would be able to help me. I knew none better than him at using the blue seed, which meant his analytical skills were far better than mine.

I glanced up at him and saw that his eyes were focused on my face. He must've noticed that I was slipping into my mind because he quickly cracked a joke about his lab. I didn't really get it, but the way he insisted on retelling it over and over till I got it forced me to laugh because he didn't try to change his wordiness once.

After dinner, I watched him as he brought the plates to the sink, and I shook my head, my eyes squinting with a grin. I loved how he always managed to calm me. He could always see when I worried and did everything he could think of to make me laugh. He liked to say that laughter was a cure to all diseases, and I believed he was right.

I moved to his side to help with the dishes, but he pushed me with his shoulder each time I tried to get close to the sink. I had to put my hand on my mouth when my laughter grew too loud, so I wouldn't wake our baby girl. When he finished, he looked into my eyes and placed a kiss on my nose before taking hold of my hand again as we moved to the couch. Though I didn't like seeing his face straighten when we entered the living room, but it was the moment of truth, and we both knew it. I sat on the couch, waiting for him to start.

"How much would I have to lose?" he asked as he paced the room.

"Hopefully only this conversation."

He nodded and pressed his blue seed before taking it out of his forehead, turning it upside down, then putting it back in place. "This will ensure that when I erase my memory after, I won't lose anything before this moment."

It always fascinated me to see how our seeds allowed us to control everything in our bodies. The blue seed controls most of our brain functions and enhances its capabilities at will, and what it couldn't control, the purple seed could.

He sat on the low table in front of me and placed his elbows on his knees, leaning forward. "I'm all ears," he said.

I nodded, taking the time to decide where to start, then jumped right in. "My new mission requires that I investigate a certain Delphian and gather information on him, but I fear that he already knows I'm going to do it. He was here for a meeting this morning and whispered to me that we would meet again."

Bodya brought his head back and placed his arms behind him. "That is indeed tricky." He took a deep breath. "Have you come up with a strategy?"

"None yet." I shook my head.

"Does your mission require that you meet him again?"

"It might. His faction was supposed to send us data on him, but they sent practically nothing. If they are hiding the information somewhere, I could, in theory, find it without ever meeting him. However, if they don't have this information, then I may need to get it out of him directly." I looked into Bodya's still face, and my eyes widened when he showed no reaction to them sharing data with us. "Did you know we exchange files with Delphia?"

He nodded.

"Do you think they have files on you and me?"

"No, this only concerns leadership positions."

"He is head of the correspondence office. I wouldn't consider that a leadership position."

"It isn't, but he is responsible for all communications between the leaders of all factions. I think the Delphian representative would also report to him and not to their leaders directly, though I'm not sure. Either way, he may not make decisions, but he communicates them. If he chooses to transfer the wrong information, it could mean war. Therefore, there has to be a file on him."

"I see." My lips twisted to the side in thought. "This mission won't be easy then."

"No, it won't." He leaned forward and took hold of my hands. "This is a position of trust. They wouldn't give it to anyone. If they said nothing about him, then there's something big behind this man. Delphians don't act hastily, and they must have known we would see a red flag in his file."

Bodya paused, closing his eyes while he took a deep breath. "I'm worried about this one."

I put my palm on his cheek and moved closer. "I am too, but I'm the best spy we have. If anyone can do it, it would be me."

"Fine." He said with a sigh and nodded. "Then, tomorrow you come with me to my lab. I might have something that could help."

"You will take me to your lab?" My grin widened.

"Only this once." He pulled his blue seed out and turned it again, locking the memory so he could erase it whenever he wanted. "But this conversation is over for tonight." He wrapped an arm around my waist and flipped me over his shoulder. He carried me to the bedroom as I pretended to struggle amidst my laughter.

SEEDS AND MEMORIES

The morning after we started for his lab, lost in each other's eyes as we walked hand in hand. Even though the building where he worked was an extension to the one where I had my office, I hardly ever went there. I smiled when he told every security check we passed that I was with him as if I didn't have a higher clearance than his.

Anyone could see my wide grin from afar, yet I was more surprised when we crossed the door leading to his division. The lab had a more retro feel to it than I expected it would. The place where most inventions came from looked more classic than one would think. I glanced at Bodya from the corner of my eye and noticed how his were glued to my face.

"What?" I smiled.

"What you?" He chuckled. "What do you think?"

"Looks old. Older than you even." I stuck my tongue out.

He laughed as he started toward the center of the room. I took a second look at the massive place, realizing that it looked bigger on the inside than it did on the outside, much bigger, in fact. I moved with a double step to catch up with him on the small metal bridge, which separated the lab in half.

"You know," Bodya said, locking his hands behind his back, "we are the only faction that has the ability to experience everything more than once for the first time.

"What is that supposed to mean?" My eyes widened as I grabbed his arm, bringing him to a stop at the edge of the bridge. "Was I here before?"

"Hey, Oran, nice to see you again."

I quickly turned to face the woman behind me as she moved toward the bridge. I inspected her several times with raised brows but had no recollection of her.

"How many times have I been here?" I turned back to Bodya.

"A few. And every time you say the same thing and stick your tongue out in the end."

I felt my face heat up and knew I must have been turning red. I believe Bodya felt it, too, because he stood there staring at me.

"I actually love it," he added, "and though I hate asking you to erase this memory at the end of each visit, I look forward to this moment every time you come here."

I continued to stare at him, saying nothing, wondering how he always found the right words to make me feel better.

"Through here." He opened a glass door to his office and motioned me inside. "Make yourself comfortable. I will be right back."

I stopped by the door and stayed there until he left before bringing my eyes to his name carved on the glass: Bodya Taman. I brushed my fingers over the letters, savoring their indentation in the glass before I moved inside. His office was all glass. He had a desk, three chairs, and a couch. I sat on the couch to test its comfort, believing this was where he slept when he had to stay for weeks on end at work. I thought it was sturdy but not good enough for a good night's sleep. I decided he needed to have a couch without a glass frame and planned to force him to get one. I moved to the other edge of the office to look at the rest of the lab through his glass walls, and that was when I saw them. The true inventions lined one after the other as if on display in a museum. My jaw dropped the same moment I heard him come back in.

"With all the cool things here, why do you stock old inventions at the entrance of the lab?" I turned to face him. "Is it to camouflage yourselves?"

He laughed. "The way to the future begins with the past."

"So, it's for decoration?"

"Partly." He sat at his desk and placed a stack of files he had brought with him on top. "Most of the other inventions are from earlier times, before we had seeds or before our seeds evolved to their current form. We study them to see if we can incorporate them within our seeds."

"So—"

"We can talk about this later," he interrupted. "I have work to do, but these are all the files we have on how the power of Delphians work. Take your time reading them, and when I return, we can discuss how we can use their power to your advantage."

I nodded and moved closer for a kiss. When he left the office again, I took the files to the couch and went through them one by one, reading each several times."

***

When Bodya next returned to his office, he seemed angry about something. I wanted to ask him what was wrong but feared that he couldn't answer. I knew he would talk to me if he wanted, so I waited in silence, giving him the chance to speak. He sat behind his desk and closed his eyes for a few seconds, taking multiple deep breaths. When he opened them again, he looked at me, and I could see he was struggling to paint a smile on his face.

"Did you read all the files?" he asked.

I nodded.

"And?"

I moved from the couch to the chair opposite him. "Here's what I understood about their power. First, Delphians can only see their own future. Second, they can see multiple timelines and differentiate between the original one and the alternates. Third, they can change the future by changing their own action. Their actions can create what they call a domino effect, but what they do has to always be the first piece in the line of dominos."

"Exactly." He nodded. "But that action could be as small as just changing a decision in their minds. It's what we know here as the butterfly effect." He locked his eyes with mine. "What else?"

"The Delphians refer to practicing their power as saiting, which means looking into the mind's eye in the language of the first civilization."

"Someone is bragging about their knowledge of dead languages." The corners of both his mouth and eyes lifted.

"It was actually written in the files."

"Right." He chuckled.

"Back to our subject," I teased him with a smile. "The average Delphian takes six point four seconds to see two weeks into the future. This is possible because their brains process time differently when they saite. However, the two weeks don't have to be a single alternate timeline. It could be fourteen alternates that last for a day or three hundred and thirty-six alternates that last an hour each. Basically, the amount of time spent saiting will result in a certain period, but they can choose to divide it, however they see fit."

"They also don't have to saite for the full period. They could investigate the future for one second or a full day if they wanted to. This number was just a guide for us to understand how it works, though it also refers to a complete circle of a perfect saite."

"What do you mean?" I raised my brows.

"A complete circle is the number of alternates they need to see to find the right timeline where they learn the action needed to change the future. That number is usually between one and two hundred. A perfect saite is one where they were successful. They believe that most actions needed could be found within six point four seconds and that if they don't find it within this time, then there was a high probability that none of their actions could change the future."

"Wouldn't that mean they don't look too far?"

"Most Delphians use their power to look only a few minutes or several hours ahead. They don't look far into the future every day."

"That makes sense, actually." I took a deep breath to organize my thoughts. "An average Delphian can see up to six months in the future, but that could increase with training. Practice can also help in shortening the six point four seconds interval, allowing them to see the same period in a shorter time."

I stared up at the ceiling, distracted by my thoughts. "I'm sorry, but I still find it weird they don't look too far into the future."

"Bear in mind that we are talking about the average Delphian. Those are the ones who graduate and accept ordinary jobs that don't require them to investigate the future. People who work in sensitive places, like soldiers, train to see further in time. This is why they have the collar system."

"Yeah, I didn't understand that part, actually."

"Collars are their ranking system. With each advancement into the future, meaning how far they can see, they also advance to a different color of collar. The average Delphian wears a white collar, for instance. Blue is for those who can see up to three years, red is for five years, brown is for a decade, and black is for a century or more. Brown is actually rare, and black is hardly ever witnessed."

"Now that you mention it, I think Matso wore a brown collar." I sighed.

Bodya moved from behind his desk to the chair opposite me. He leaned forward and put my hand in his. "Don't let time scare you." He looked into my eyes. "Matso's power would still work the same way, and we won't leave here before we have the perfect plan."

I nodded, attempting to force a smile, but failed.

"On to the next." He rested his back against the chair and waited for me to continue.

"Delphians get tired from excessive saiting. Their brains go numb, and they lose the ability to sleep. They combat this with meditation, sport, and medications."

"Good. I think we've covered what they can do. Perhaps we should look into what they can't do."

"They can't see a future where they aren't present. For example, if a Delphian sees himself meeting me in the future, they wouldn't be able to see what I do while I'm not with them."

"Yeah, but this part is tricky."

"How?"

"You have to remember that they are sneaky and masters in manipulation. Because the alternate timelines change based on their decisions, they can see how the future would be for situations when they aren't present."

My eyes widened as I signaled him to explain more.

"For example, if you were with a Delphian and left to meet someone else. They could saite to see themselves following you, which would allow them to see where you go, who you meet, and what you say even if they won't do it in the end."

"That is a dangerous power. What you're saying means someone could have already listened to our current conversation."

"Not this one because they wouldn't be able to pass security. If they meet an obstacle that prevents them from completing the timeline, they won't see it. However, theoretically, they could if we had no security or if they knew how to bypass it."

"Still, communication with Lunar would be impossible while I'm there."

"Not necessarily. You will just need to be alert and always make sure no one could tail you, even if there were no one."

"There are too many factors to consider, too many hoops to jump through. This mission is getting harder, not easier."

Bodya tapped on his blue seed twice. I understood what he wanted to do and did the same with mine. The double-tap allowed us to access our brains and increase their capacity by two hundred percent. We both closed our eyes as we surfed all the information, untangling and analyzing everything. Ten minutes later, I opened my eyes.

"We have been looking at this from the wrong angle," I said, alerting him before he opened his own eyes.

"Did you find a solution?" he asked.

"I'm not really sure."

"Let's examine what your mind came up with then." He rested his elbow on his desk.

I straightened my posture. "We have been searching for a way to bypass the Delphians' power, so they won't see what I'm up to, which so far seems impossible."

He leaned slightly forward, paying close attention to my next words.

"Instead, we should find a way to make them see what we want them to see. Use their power to our advantage."

"I like the concept. Making them see what we want them to see will not just keep them off your tail but would also cement their trust in you. However, the problem will remain in the alternates. The Delphians have had this power for almost a thousand years, and they know its ins and outs. They know what to change in their minds so they can generate a different reaction from you, unless…" Bodya stopped mid-sentence and stood to pace the room as his blue seed blinked rapidly. I waited for him to decipher his thoughts.

He halted in the middle of the room and turned to face me. "If you didn't know what they're looking for, they would never find it."

"I like where you're going." I smiled. "But I'm not sure I fully understand."

He returned to his seat. "When you came here today, I knew what you were going to say at the entrance because I saw it happen many times, but you didn't know."

My eyes widened.

"Regardless of the number of times you've been here, you reacted the same way to the same thing because that is who you are. We learn by experiment. We try something, and it fails, so we try a different thing and so on until we find what works, but if we were immediately to forget the results after we see them, then no matter how many times we repeat the experiment, we would always try the same thing because our knowledge didn't change."

"And you want to change what I know?"

He nodded.

"How would you do that?"

"By making you forget." He rested his back against his seat.

"I assume you want me to forget about the mission." I studied his grin and knew he was formulating a plan, but I was still skeptical. "How would I carry out my mission if I didn't know I had one in the first place?"

His smile filled his entire face. "By using my latest invention."

He moved toward the door and asked me to wait as if I would go anywhere else. I had no idea how his invention would help, but his enthusiasm brought hope to my heart. However, fear found its way through as well. The idea of forgetting didn't sit well with me this time, but before it could take over my mind, Bodya returned. In his hand, there was a blue rectangular-shaped box slightly larger than his palm.

He sat in the chair opposite me and raised the box in my direction. "This is the answer to all our problems. With it, you can forget and remember whatever you want."

My eyes bulged at the concept. Never in the history of our faction had someone been able to recall memories they erased. I looked up at him with pride coursing through my veins. My husband was indeed a genius, and whatever he had inside the box was a breakthrough that deserved the highest praise.

He opened the box, and in it, there were six glass seeds identical to our blue one. Only the ones in the box were smaller.

"Each of these seeds contains a memory gene similar to the one in our birth seeds. When you connect the small seed to your original one, your seed will think it's a part of you, but you will still be able to recognize it as a separate one. You can then transfer memories from your brain to this seed and store them there. When you remove the seed, you won't have any recollection of these memories. But," he said, his grin widening, "when you put it back, you also transfer all of your memories back, just as if you never lost them."

"This is amazing." I felt my heart jump with excitement. "When is it going to be public?"

"Not any time soon."

My head jerked to the back.

"This was extremely expensive to make, and the seeds can't be transferred from one person to another." He lowered his chin. "Our seeds carry our unique genetic markers. When you connect the box seeds to one, it will configure itself to the person's DNA and won't work with any other seed. On top of that, each seed can save up to one year of memories, nothing more."

"That's still six years with a box set."

"True." He nodded. "However, they could also be a threat to our security if someone used them to hide information from the protectors."

"I see. Would you be able to allow me to use them, though?"

"Yes, I will assign you as a test subject to see whether the memory seeds have a side effect or not."

"Do they?" I narrowed my eyes. "Have a side effect?"

He looked into my eyes with a slow shake of his head. "I don't know. We tried the first set, and there was nothing, but it was only for a few hours. I don't know if something would happen to the memories if they remained separated for a long time." He looked at the panic in my eyes and squeezed my hand. "It should be okay. My calculations say there would be nothing wrong."

I nodded, although my heart trembled inside my chest. "So how will we do it? The plan?"

"For now, we will just register you for the test program. Then we will think about the plan tonight at home."

I studied his face, feeling mine heat up. The idea was promising, but something made me feel uneasy. I couldn't understand it but couldn't shake it away either.

A PLAN WORTHY OF A SPY

I waited with Bodya in the director's office for nearly half an hour before he joined us.

"Did you get my request?" I asked the moment he passed through the door.

"Good afternoon to you too, Oran." He moved to his chair behind his desk.

"I'm sorry." I lowered my head. "We haven't slept for two days."

"Don't worry about it." The director shook Bodya's hand before taking a seat behind his desk. "So, you want Bodya as your mission handler?"

"I do."

"I will give you the benefit of the doubt and ask directly, why? I hope it's not because he is your husband. This is a dangerous mission, and he has no experience in our work, neither in nor off the field. No offense," he added, quickly turning to face Bodya.

"None taken, but I promise you it has nothing to do with us being married to one another. We talked about it, and I'm the best one to handle Oran's plan."

"So, you came up with a plan?" The director turned to me with a wide grin.

"We did." I nodded. "It's risky and has no room for error, but we think we can do it."

"Tell me your plan then, and I will tell you if he can be your handler or not, but keep in mind that in the end, we will discuss the fact that you spoke about a secret mission with someone outside this office." He turned to Bodya. "Again, no offense."

Bodya chuckled. "Again, none taken." He pulled out the box of memory seeds and placed it open on the desk. "Do you know what this is?" he asked the director.

"Invention three five two one, a memory container. I'm one of the five people who get to know about all your work, and I have to say, you are a talented scientist. Perhaps one of the best."

"Thank you." Bodya tilted his head. "We will use those memory containers for the mission."

"How?"

"We will erase some of Oran's memories and inject fake ones to control her behavior."

"Walk me through the full plan, please. I don't want to connect the pieces myself."

I raised my hand to signal Bodya to let me speak before he opened his mouth again. "We will erase any memory I have about the mission, and I will remember only the meeting we had with the Delphians. We will then inject memories of you giving me a mission to investigate the Kalangous instead like I said during the meeting. But that mission will fail, and you will turn against me. Or at least, that is what I must believe. After that, you will put me in prison as a punishment. However, we must stage the following sequence in a way that makes me lose hope in my faction and find myself in a position where I must escape, with Delphia being my only option for survival."

"And how would you carry your mission if you don't remember it?"

Bodya placed his hand on the desk. "As a scientist, I can visit Delphia to check on the machines we gave them as part of the maintenance personnel. First, we will wait until her asylum is clear, and they give her their trust, then I will give her part of her memories back. Enough to entice her about investigating Matso, but not too much so she wouldn't be in danger. Each time she passes a milestone, I will give her more memories to help her in the next phase, and so on."

50

"And how do you plan to inject her with the fake memories?" The director placed his arms on his desk, one palm on top of the other. "Did you invent a device that adds false memories too?"

"No." Bodya shook his head. "But what is it that makes our minds believe whether something was real or fake? Context. We will enact the things we want Oran to believe and then erase the context, forcing her mind to see those memories as a standalone. She will believe it is real."

"And you want me to play an actor in this indie movie of yours?"

I laughed. "Is this what you're worried about, boss?"

He looked at me with a smile. "I knew you were crazy and would come up with an unbelievable solution, but I didn't know that your husband was as crazy as you."

Bodya reached for my hand and locked his eyes with mine. "A level of craziness is required in every job that needs creativity."

"I see why he needs to be your handler for this mission," said the director. "However, I have to note a flaw in your plan." He shook his head. "The Oran I know would never escape even if it meant her death, not while her family is here."

I moved my lips to the side as I lowered my head. My heart raced, and my breathing became ragged until Bodya cradled my hand with his. I took a deep breath and turned to the director. "I can't have a family while I'm on this mission. We looked at all the possibilities, and if the Delphians found out that I have a family, they could use it against me. But more importantly, you are right. If I remembered my family, I would never leave Lunar. This would be my instinct, and we have to make sure it's not how I would behave."

"You want to erase your family too?" The director's eyes bulged out. "That means the last four years of your life."

"Five and a half," I quickly added. "Five and a half years ago, we had an argument and broke up for three days. We will make it appear as if we never got back together."

The director rested his back against his chair. "You're crazier than I thought. In fact, I don't think the word crazy is enough to describe you."

Bodya focused his gaze on me. "It will only be for a short time. A year maximum."

"Wouldn't she feel that there are too many holes in her memory?"

"Not really." Bodya shook his head. "We don't think about memories all the time, only when we want to recall something, and even then, it's usually something specific that pops into our heads due to external factors. Even if someone asked her directly about what she did at a certain time, she would just find it weird that she can't remember it. Worst case, she will think it was something bad, and she had to remove it, but she won't question the rest of her memories because her identity won't be in question. She will also have memories of the last five years and remember her training and missions, just not anything with our daughter or me in it."

"I see." The director rocked his chair. "Are you sure you want to do this?"

"Yes. I'm sure." I looked into my husband's eyes.

"And you Bodya? Since this will affect you too, and you would be part of this mission."

"I'm with Oran wherever she goes." He looked at me with a smile, one that calmed all my senses. I wished at that moment that there was no mission, that I didn't need to forget about him or my daughter, but I knew that as long as he was by my side, everything was possible.

"I love you." I mouthed, but I think the director saw it anyway.

"Go spend more time together then while you still know each other, and I will organize everything here, and with Kala, then I will call you back in a week or two."

I looked at the director with narrowed eyes. "I thought you said I had four days to start the mission, and you only need like two or three more to organize everything."

"I just gave you an extension, and technically, this mission has already started."

I thanked him and nodded before I left his office. I could sense he felt bad for us and added the days just so we would have more time together, and I was grateful for that.

THE SHORES OF LUNAR

When the director gave me the extra days, Bodya took a vacation from his work and insisted that we take our daughter and go away for some family-only time. We left Lunar the capital, and traveled to Lunar Three. Three, like all our cities, looked almost identical to the capital with matching architecture and spirit. However, Three had one significant difference that made it attractive to tourists, its shores had large natural waves. This is because Three was the last island in Lake Zuno and the nearest to the eastern mountains of Mastoperia, which concentrated a constant stream of wind above the surface of the water.

Like every other visitor, we headed to the beach on a perfectly sunny day with a sky as blue as my daughter's eyes. The weather was also right, with a little touch of heat that we could soften in the lake. But what made the day worth it was the smile on Bodya's face and Evailen's laughter.

"Do you remember when we came here for our honeymoon?" Bodya asked while plunging the umbrella into the ground.

"I do," I answered, spreading a piece of cloth in the shade before sitting and resting Evailen on my lap. "I also remember all the other vacations we spent on this very beach. We ought to find a new place to discover."

Bodya chuckled. "What's better than the waves?" He took Evailen off my hands and lifted her to his shoulders. "Right?" he asked her. "You like the water too, don't you?"

"Yes, Papa."

"Of course, she does." I rolled my eyes. "It's her first time."

Bodya kept his eyes on Evailen and spoke only to her. "No, it isn't. You came here before when you were in Mama's belly."

Chuckling, I rose to my feet and pulled my daughter off his shoulders. "Don't listen to your father. Only Mama knows what's best."

"Papa knows too," Evailen said, frowning.

"No, Evailen. Repeat after me. Papa knows nothing."

"No," she said with conviction. "Papa knows too."

"Come on, my love. Say it, and I will take you to Lunar Seven. They have the largest theme park in our faction and with characters from all your favorite games."

"Papa will take me."

Bodya laughed out loud, and I narrowed my eyes at Evailen. "I thought we were best friends, Eva. How can you leave me hanging like this?"

"I don't leave you hagny, Mama. I love you too."

"You do?" My grin widened. "How much?"

"That much." She spread her arms wide.

"Then why don't you want to repeat after me."

She wrapped her arms around me and leaned closer to my ear, then started whispering. "Papa knows all chatactas on my wall and promised he will take me to see them for my next bitsday."

"Did he?" I gave Bodya a look.

"With your permission, of course, love," Bodya quickly added, then rushed to kiss my cheeks before carrying me by my waist with Evailen still in my arms and running to the water. Evailen started laughing, and even though I could tell he was doing it to change the subject, I found myself laughing too. When he let go of us in the water, I lowered Evailen until her shoulders were submerged, and the two of us splashed Bodya, who pretended to be drowning.

When we got tired of the lake, we spread out under the umbrella, Bodya's hand in mine with Evailen playing in the sand next to us.

"This is perfect," I said, looking at the blue sky. "I wish I didn't have to leave."

"It is, but what makes it perfect is that we only get to taste it every now and then. If this moment was to last forever, it would become tasteless."

"Bodya, the philosopher." I turned my head in his direction. "This is what you should have done with your life, not become a scientist."

He turned to me, meeting my eyes. "There's philosophy in science too, but what matters is that it's my passion, the same way spying is yours." He scooched his shoulders closer. "I know that you are afraid about this mission. I won't lie, I am too, but I also know that you won't be happy if you don't try, and I'd rather you take the risk if it will fulfill you rather than living with the doubt for the rest of your life."

"I love you, Bodya, with every cell in my body."

His cheeks turned red. "I love you too, but I do it with my heart." He winked at me then kissed my lips.

***

The director, Bodya, and I sat in the meeting room with four protectors standing in a line opposite us. They were in a military pose, wearing their blue leather uniforms, their armors covering half their bodies.

"Now," the director said to the protectors. "You must do everything I said to the letter. Mess it up, and I will mess your entire lives. Is that clear?"

The four nodded before the director turned to me. "Anything you want to add?" he asked.

Rising to my feet, I walked to one of the men in line and asked him to handcuff me.

"Too comfy, and I can escape it with ease," I said. "Make it tighter."

The protector did as I said, but I kept asking for more until I grunted.

"Take it easy on her," Bodya said, leaning forward with a sudden move.

"No." I shook my head. "It needs to be even tighter. I have to believe they are serious about punishing me, so I lose faith in the system."

My husband sighed but leaned back, uttering nothing, leaving me in control of the situation. After I gave them a few more orders and tested all four of them, I gave my approval to the director, who told them to leave and meet him later for more instructions. After that, we left the room and moved to my boss's office for some final details.

When everything was in order, and I was ready, Bodya took my hand and pulled me to a corner in the office. He grabbed my other hand and looked into my eyes. "Oran, I will support you no matter what, but I have to give you a chance to back out and ask. Are you sure you want to do this mission?"

I took a deep breath and exhaled it loudly, then looked into his eyes for a silent minute before finally nodding. "I know the risk, but this is what I'm good at, and like you said, I have to know if I can break the Delphians and defeat them at their own game."

"Okay, but if anything goes wrong, I will pull you out."

I nodded a second time.

"Alright," the director said. "It's time. We set every clock and calendar in the building to make it look like the day of the meeting with Matso, but we need to start now, or we will have to set up everything again."

"Okay, okay," I said and walked out of the office, Bodya behind me.

In the corridor, he kissed my hand, my cheek, then my lips. "I love you, Oran, and when you are back, I promise to say it every day so you can never forget it again."

I smiled, a tear on the side of my eyes, but I told myself that it was my choice and I needed to remain strong. "I love you too," I said, then repeated the phrase four more times before we kissed again.

"Alright," he stepped back, and our hands remained touching until our fingers became out of reach. "Once I go, erase the memories you marked with my colleague yesterday from your brain, and everything should start on its own."

Nodding, I bit my lips and focused my gaze on him as he continued to walk backward while looking at me. And just as he was about to turn away, he threw me a kiss in the air but left me no time to do the same.

I heaved a heavy sigh and wiped the few tears that tried to escape, then closed my eyes. After tapping my blue seed, I concentrated on my mind and removed the memories we agreed upon from my brain, leaving no trace of the last two weeks. When I opened my eyes again, the mission had begun.

PART TWO

Again, and From the Top

SOLO MISSION

I paced back and forth in front of the director's office, waiting for the moment I could go inside. The red seed on the left side of my chest blinked quickly as my heart raced. I wasn't sure how I felt about this turn of events, but I convinced myself I was excited. The moment the hologram of a watch around my wrist ticked the right time, I knocked and entered the director's office, even before he gave me permission.

He was behind his desk, going through a stack of papers, and appeared to be reading each of them carefully. When I approached the desk, he motioned for me to sit. I sat opposite him rocking my feet as I waited for him to speak.

"Relax. I will tell you everything." His eyes remained focused on the words he was reading.

"So? Will you send me to Kala to investigate the new council as I suggested?" The corners of my eyes lifted in question.

Nodding, he tidied his stack of papers and placed them in his office drawer before locking it with his thumbprint. "You were right. The Kalangous power is becoming too dangerous for us to ignore. A few of them have always been able to stand their ground against many, but for one man to defeat an entire tribe..." He paused, fidgeting with his ring. "We have to once again ask questions that we long agreed to leave unanswered."

"What will you have me do?" I asked, leaning toward his desk.

"It's time to know how their power really works. If we can find the source, then we can have the upper hand."

"You want me to find the gates?"

He nodded. "We need to know where they are and how they work. We must either learn their magic or know how to destroy their connection with these gates."

My eyes widened. "You don't want to wipe them off the face of Mastoperia, do you?"

He chuckled. "Not at all, but as you said in the meeting, we can't let them continue to get stronger while we stand and watch. I just want us to be ready if there was ever another war."

"I totally agree, but I will need a team. I have been in Kala many times and never found a sign of these gates. It looks like I will have to infiltrate their Red Temple, and it won't be easy."

"No." He shook his head. "This mission will be off the books, and I can't risk the lives of an entire team. You are my best spy. This is why I'm assigning the mission to you. However, I understand that what I'm asking is highly dangerous, and you can refuse the mission if you want. I won't hold it against you."

My red seed started blinking again, indicating that my emotions were out of control, but I was a spy, a master of controlling myself. I took a deep breath and cleared my mind, turning my emotions to mere thoughts that I could contain in the blue seed on the left side of my forehead. The director's grin widened, and I was sure he was enjoying seeing me put my feelings under control.

"So?" he asked.

"I will do it," I answered quickly. "None has ever infiltrated the Red Temple. It's a challenge I won't pass on, and as you said, I'm your best spy. If I can't do it, then no one can."

"That's why you are my favorite, Oran. You never shy away from a hard mission. It's no wonder you rose through the ranks faster than anyone else."

I was sure there was no better spy in all of Lunar, but I still wondered if my skill would be enough to infiltrate Kala's most guarded place. I shook my head, pushing the thoughts away and turned back to the director. "Let's talk logistics then. What can you offer me?"

"Nothing," he answered. "I already told you that we won't recognize anything you do. Oran, if Kala catches you, you will be on your own. You do understand that, right?"

"Yes, yes. I meant information or at least technology. We have an entire department tasked with building the latest gadgets for our line of work. Are you saying there's nothing new you can offer?"

"Even if there is, I won't give it to you. It will be you and your six seeds for this mission. I can't risk our inventions falling in their hands either."

My eyes slightly narrowed as I wondered if the director was okay with giving me up.

"Of course, it's not okay to lose you either," he said.

My brows drew together. "I didn't say anything."

"I didn't become the director by listening only to what people say out loud. It's written all over your face."

"Then I didn't do a good job at hiding my thoughts."

"Don't beat yourself up about it. I don't expect you to be a spy all the time. You are entitled to relax, at least while you're not working."

I pursed my lips. "Fine. Is there anything I need to know about Kala, at least?"

"We don't have much, really. As usual, Kala still lives in the old age. Their faction doesn't really change like ours. However, their new council chose to mask their identity from the rest of the world. We have no idea who they are. In fact, if you can find out anything about them, it will be great, but consider this to be a bonus mission. It's not your primary objective."

With a nod, I rose to my feet. "I will leave—"

The director raised his hand, interrupting my words. "From this point forward, it's best that I know nothing. As far as I'm concerned, you are on official leave. And Oran..." he took his blue seed out of his forehead and turned it, then put it back in place.

I nodded one more time and started toward the exit without uttering a word. I knew what his action meant. He had obviously done the same thing before I entered his office. By twisting the seed back, he would be able to use its power to control his memory, erasing our conversation from his mind. If the protectors of our faction were to investigate his memories later, they would find no trace of our conversation. Even *he* wouldn't know about it. It was clear that from the moment our discussion ended, I was completely on my own, like he said.

However, as I stepped out of the director's office, something happened, something that instantly redirected my train of thought. I bumped into Bodya. For a moment, our eyes met, and he smiled at me, but I instantly turned away and started walking with fast steps. It had been years since I saw Bodya, yet this glance riled my emotions. I was angry at myself as I realized that my red seed was blinking again, and this time, it didn't stop even after I took several deep breaths. I was mad at myself for still carrying feelings toward someone who broke up with me over five years prior, and I began to feel that anger pulsing through my body.

To calm myself, I ran through the corridors, down the stairs, and out of the building, then continued with the same speed across my city all the way to my apartment, three miles away.

My eyes narrowed a little as I entered my flat. I wasn't sure why I even lived in such a boring place. Its gray walls were bland, vacant of any decoration. The light was nearly absent and heightened only by the one bulb hanging from my living room ceiling. I had a small white table with a single chair opposite it, and as I turned my gaze to the open kitchen, I realized I had no more than a single plate and an equal number of utensils. Even the paint smelled fresh, as if I was coming into the apartment for the first time.

It had been five years since I moved into this place, yet it never felt like home, only a stopover to rest a little between missions. I was angered by my place for no apparent reason, and I began to believe it was because of running into Bodya.

I had never been with anyone since him, and I wished I could still take him in my arms. My brain drifted to how Bodya's green eyes radiated a happiness that matched his smile when I saw him.

Ugh. I grunted at myself and stepped out of the apartment again. If I couldn't be happy in my own home, then it was time to start my mission. That way, my brain wouldn't have the time to think about anything else.

Once I was back on the street, I pulled my pod out of my yellow seed and rode it, bringing myself higher than my four-story building, using my thoughts to direct the pod. Once there was nothing to block my movement, I aimed west, the direction of Kala.

THE LAND OF MAGIC

When I launched my pod toward Kala, I noticed that the sun was about to set. Usually, it took my lotus ten hours to cover the two thousand miles distance separating my faction from theirs. However, at this rate, I knew I would make it by sunrise, so I pushed my pod to its maximum speed.

I grabbed onto the petal-like edges as my speed reached three hundred and fifty miles per hour. My shoulder-length black hair flapped behind my head as my eyes narrowed to battle the strong wind crashing against my face. Within minutes of flying at top speed, my brain started to feel numb, and I was getting a little high, so I focused on my blue and black seeds. Using my thoughts, I manipulated the movement of my blood, pumping more of it into my brain to stay focused on the road ahead, especially after it became dark, and all I had was the light of the stars to guide me since the moon was absent that night.

A little after midnight, I was standing outside Kala's stone walls, plotting an infiltration to find the location of their magical gates and hopefully collect information on their new council.

It wasn't the first time I broke through their defenses. Other than a few patrols that seem to only care about large attacks and could be easily avoided by flying high enough, Kala didn't pay much attention to spy activity. They have walls around their villages, but they only man the gates.

I remembered the first time I broke in. I was surprised by how easy it was, but I quickly realized the reason they didn't really care. Kala is a simple faction. If one lived their whole life inside one of their villages, they would think our world was still in its medieval era, perhaps even before then. Their secrets are in their hearts. There is no paper trail to track or technology to hack. They, and the other faction that controls animals, Averett, live in a world of their own, separate from anything else. Well, at least the Averettis have a sense of humor. Not the Kalangous, though. They are always preparing for the next fight as if there is nothing in the world but battle.

That night, I snuck into their main village the same way I always did, by climbing their rock wall, only six hundred feet away from the main gate. I made it inside undetected, but I had to break into a place I never could before: the Red Temple, the only place they guard. It is where their council lives, and if I had to bet voins on where the gates would be, I would put it all on that ancient construction. The temple has an outer wall of its own, protecting an open yard and a massive stone structure with four towers, one at each corner. The Red Temple is also their highest construction, visible from everywhere in the village, even from outside the main walls.

Hiding in a dark spot, I clicked my heels together and brushed my purple seed before my outfit changed to resemble their wide tunics. Their cultural clothes were perfect because, with a scarf on top, I could hide all my seeds and walk around as if I was one of them. It didn't matter much, though. There was hardly anyone out in the streets. It looked as if the whole village went to sleep early.

When I saw the temple directly in front of me, I hid behind a haystack and watched the guards from a distance, counting how long it took them to circle the walls. There were twelve guards in groups of two, all with long spears. I thought the weapons were odd for people who used magic, especially since they never relied on such blades in battle, but I wasn't there to investigate their weapon of choice.

After careful observation, I learned that the longest free interval between the guards was fifty seconds. I waited for the fourth time the interval was open before I ran toward the stone structure. I clicked my heels another time when I got to the wall, and the iron in my blood crawled outside my skin before transforming into gloves that covered my hands. I then manipulated the glove, using my thoughts again to give myself tiny grapple hooks at the tips of my fingers.

The wall wasn't high, and I climbed it quickly. As I reached the top of the wall, I saw two guards turn a corner that led them to me, so I quickly rolled my body to fall on the other side. I had time for just a split second's glance and saw no one in the temple court. Like a cat, I landed on my feet, but when I tried to take my first step after, I couldn't.

I looked down and saw vines turning around my legs, holding me in place, but there was still no one around, as far as I could see, so I dug for a knife in my pocket and started to cut through the vines. But each time I cut one, two others latched onto me. I followed the vines to find their origin, but they seemed to originate from a long branch that disappeared into the darkness of the night.

A few seconds later, I heard footsteps approach. I prepared to fight, believing that whoever was coming could see me, even though I couldn't see them, and then there was light.

A tall, bald man, black as the night, stood by the temple's second entrance, a fireball floating above his palm. I had studied Kala's magic when I was training for my job, so I knew he was using the power of the fourth gate to conjure and control the elements. I wasn't sure if the vines were part of the elements they could control, but there was no one else around. It had to have been his magic.

My hands were free. I could have brushed my black seed to launch my armor and weapons and fight that man, but I knew the other guards would hear us. Thirteen against one wouldn't be a fair fight. Hiding wasn't an option either since the fire in his hand would surely give him a better vision radiance than mine, so I decided to follow a different tactic.

I straightened and leaned toward the light, waving at him. When his eyes fell on me, I spoke with a voice that was barely above a whisper. "I have a message for you to give your council."

The man said nothing. He approached me, coming close enough that I could see the fire reflected in his black eyes. He brought his fire-holding hand close to my face and removed my scarf before turning around.

"Follow me," he said.

"I can't. These things around my legs are holding me still."

He stopped and turned only his head to look at me. "You can now. They will stay around your leg, though, in case you try to run away." He then continued toward the heart of the temple, and I followed him in silence.

The vines were heavy, and they turned my gait into a limp. I didn't ask any questions because I knew he was taking me to whomever I could talk to. We passed through three rooms inside the temple before he waited for me to catch up and stand by his side. Then he waved his hand, and the door to the fourth room moved on its own.

He pointed inside. "Go in."

The vines fell onto the floor as soon as I walked through the door and saw the six members who seemed to be waiting for me. They were covered in wide tunics that hid their entire bodies. Even their faces were scarfed, and I could only see their eyes. They were the members of Kala's council.

"What are you doing here?" asked one of the council members.

At first, I wasn't sure who spoke, but I deduced that it was one of the two in the center.

"I won't ask again."

Hearing the voice again, I concluded the speaker was the third one from the right, the tallest among the six.

I turned my gaze to him. "I was just fascinated with your ancient architecture and wanted to take a closer look."

"You should have come during the day then. You would be able to see it clearly."

I tilted my head. "I'm more of a night person. I like to see the reflection of the moon on art."

"Did you ever see its reflection on blood?"

I narrowed my eyes, confused by his words. I wasn't sure if he was making a bad joke or genuinely asking, but somehow it felt like a threat. I examined their body language, but none of them had moved a muscle, and they all stood in the same pose. Clearly, something they did many times and were comfortable repeating.

I had to push him to get more information, but I needed to be coy about it. A small conversation should do it. "What kind of blood are we talking about?" I faked a smile.

"Yours."

"Well—"

"I have had enough of this," he interrupted, clapping his hands, then the door opened again.

My brows curled at how fast he dropped the conversation, but I couldn't push on him. Someone who acted like that was either crazy in their head or knew exactly what they were doing. I glanced behind me, and the guard who brought me in was still standing there, in a pose similar to the council members.

"Mydon," the old man said, "take her out of the city, then execute and bury her. We had no visitors tonight."

My eyes widened, and I glanced back and forth between the guard and the council members. I moved my hand to the black seed atop the right side of my chest to activate my weapon, but before I could reach it, the vines were all over my body, blocking my every movement.

My heart raced, and I began to sweat. Kala was the last place I wanted to die.

THE DEVIL'S EYES

The guard, Mydon, moved his hand, and the vines lifted me above the ground before hovering me behind him as he walked out of the temple. Knowing we would be alone soon, I decided to wait until we were far from his faction before I worked on freeing myself. Fighting one enemy would be much easier, and he was doing me a favor by separating himself from his backup. However, my eyes widened when I saw where we headed. Instead of leaving the faction, we walked into the garden of a home, a simple house made of mud bricks, decorated with imperfect images of what I assumed to be fictional Kalangou characters. The portraits seemed to be painted by children or someone who struggled with their talents. They were also filled with contradicting colors, but it may have been a night effect.

When we reached the house door, he brought my feet to the ground. "I'm going to drop the vines to your legs again, but if you try to make any sudden moves, I will drive them through your heart faster than you can blink."

I nodded in the small space I could move my head before most of the vines faded in the wind, leaving me capable of moving again.

He stepped into the house, and I followed, fueled by curiosity. Everything I knew about Kalangous indicated that they never break their superiors' orders. It was also the first time for me inside one of their houses without the need to be quiet or watch my step.

Inside, the living room was simple. As usual, there was no sign of technology or anything beyond the second century of the new age. Their furniture was only what a basic person needed to survive, and even the decorations remained simple and clearly handmade.

He lit a few candle torches around the room before I heard a voice.

"Papa?" The voice of a little girl came from upstairs. "Are you back?"

"Yes, my darling," Mydon answered as he continued to light the rest of the candles.

The girl ran down the stairs, barefoot and in one-piece pajamas. She ran to her father and jumped on him so he would carry her. She couldn't be more than five or six, and she kept blasting his cheeks with kisses.

A few seconds later, a woman with onyx-colored skin, black eyes, and wearing a green nightgown appeared atop the stairs.

"Easy on your father, my dear," the woman said to the girl as she descended.

"It's okay." Mydon chuckled before he put his daughter down.

When she reached the living room, the woman studied me until her eyes fell on the vines around my leg. After that, she ignored me and moved to Mydon.

"A new mission?" she asked him.

He nodded as he put a teapot on a stove with a flat metal surface and a hole in the middle for burning wood.

"Will you be back soon?" the woman asked in a calm tone.

"Just a couple of days."

"Be careful." She placed her palm on his chest and leaned in for a kiss, then carried the little girl up the stairs.

I followed her movement with my eyes and noticed a boy sitting on the last step. He must have been somewhere between eight and ten, and his eyes focused on me. They were young but scary. I could feel his hatred flowing through his stare, and I didn't want to know what happened to him to harbor all that darkness at his age, but the woman took hold of his hand when she reached him and led him somewhere that I couldn't see.

74

I glanced back at Mydon, who now had two cups of tea in his hands. He placed them on a table in the middle of the room and sat down on a wooden chair before signaling for me to sit on the other side.

When I joined him at the table, he pushed one of the teacups toward me.

"I'm not a fan of tea, but thank you," I said.

He lifted his cup and sipped some of it, saying nothing. I didn't know why, but I felt like I owed him, so I lifted the cup and took a sip. It was too sweet for my taste but warm enough to battle their cold desert.

"Aren't you going to kill me?" I raised my eyes to look at him.

He remained silent, but a slight shake from his head gave me the answer.

"Are you in a quarrel with your council? Is this why you're defying their order?"

He stared at me with the same deadly quietness for a few seconds, and I guessed he was contemplating his answer. "Questions like this may force me to kill you unless this was why you invaded my faction. Do you want to die?"

"I don't," I quickly answered, but he was right. I couldn't play spy at this moment. The Kalangous are secretive and carry their faction with the utmost pride. Even if he were against his council, he wouldn't tell me. Maybe he had his reasons to help me, but he would definitely keep the matter internal. "Thank you," I said. It was the only good thing I knew to say.

When he finished his tea, he stood and carried his cup to the sink. "You can take a nap on the couch behind you if you want. We will leave at first light."

"And you?" I asked before he stopped and turned to face me. "Where will you sleep?" I could see a little of his smirk as he started toward the kitchen again.

I understood that he wasn't going to sleep as long as I was around. I wanted to ask him where he planned to take me but felt he wouldn't answer.

The thing that baffled me was when he said we would leave at first light. It was as if he didn't care about getting caught. I thought maybe he had accomplices at the gate who wouldn't tell his council that he waited till the morning to take me out of the faction, or maybe the council already knew that was what he would do. Still, something wasn't right, and I felt the need to know what it was, but this wasn't the right moment.

I told myself I could sneak back in after escaping. The next time though, I wouldn't break into the temple but follow him. He was the lead I needed to untangle some of their secrets.

For now, all I could do was rest, so I decided to take his advice and moved to the couch for a nap. The morning was going to come either way, and I would find out then what he intended to do with me.

A JOURNEY TO HELL

The following morning, he surprisingly removed all his vines from around my body, erasing each from existence. When he did it, his eyes remained focused on me, and I could tell he watched to see if I would attempt to run away. However, I was too intrigued by his action to escape, and I knew that if I wanted to get any information out of him, this moment was my chance. Meeting his eyes, I nodded, and we walked toward the gates of Kala together. The streets were reclaiming their life even though it was so early, yet no one paid attention to me. There were two guards at the gate, but they didn't comment on my existence either, even though they could see my seeds. The only words that came out of their mouths were a good morning greeting. I wasn't sure if they included me, so I said nothing.

We marched for a few minutes into the desert before Mydon stopped. He clutched his fist, leaving his thumb exposed before he used it to trace an imaginary three against his chest. I knew what he did allowed him to open the third gate of magic to use its power. I brought my index finger to my black seed, preparing to launch my armor instantly.

"Relax," he said. "I told you, I won't kill you."

He waved his hand toward the ground and conjured a plank of wood that he sat on. "Climb on. We will move faster like this."

I sat in the space available behind him and watched as he waved his hand to raise the wood above the ground. We were about thirty feet up in the sky before we started to move forward. The direction he took me in led to my faction, but it would also lead to the Forbidden Palace. It was at that moment that I realized he could be taking me to the Illicitums. He wouldn't be killing me as he said, but he would be condemning me to the fate I fear the most.

I had to ask. "Where are we going?"

"To your home faction." He turned his body to face me, and I understood he wanted to talk.

"What's up?" I asked with a smile, trying to lighten the mood.

"Here is the thing." He looked into my eyes, his expression serious. "Your faction sold you out."

My eyes bulged, and my heart raced, but I said nothing, waiting for what words would follow.

"We knew that you were coming, and we deliberately created a longer interval between the guards to attract you to that spot. We were watching you from afar from the moment you landed in our desert and all while you snuck into the faction. We knew exactly where you would infiltrate the temple, and I was waiting for you the whole time." He paused. "According to your people, you broke their rules, and they want nothing to do with you anymore."

"They told you that?" My breathing became more hardened with every breath. There was no way the director sold me out. I did nothing wrong.

"They said if we caught you, we could do whatever we want with you, and they won't seek revenge for your blood."

I dropped back against the flying wood, leaving my head to hang below the edge. Nothing he said made sense. Why would the director give me a mission doomed to fail? I scanned the desert below us as it moved quickly from an upside-down view. I couldn't believe that my faction would do this to me. Even if my people thought I did something wrong, which I didn't, they should have put me on trial for it rather than trick me like this. They should have charged me first and waited for a judge to pronounce my sentence. I shook my head in disbelief that Lunar would break its own rules and do this to one of their own. However, it was also strange that Kala was the merciful faction in this scenario. They weren't exactly known for being nice to their enemies, and they saw the whole world as their nemesis.

Using the strength of my upper body, I pushed myself back up. "If you have the chance to do whatever you want with me, then why give me back to my faction? Forgive my rudeness, but your faction is not exactly known for its diplomacy."

"You're right, we are not, but the council thought about it, and they don't exactly trust your faction. We just came out of a war where we lost a full council, good people that everyone loved. The old council leader, Rakamai, wanted peace, and we want to honor his wish."

Mydon took a deep breath. "We don't know if your people were honest or if this is a trap. Maybe you are a pawn they chose to sacrifice, and maybe you volunteered for the mission, though seeing your reactions, I doubt it. Either way, the risk is high, and we don't want to take it. Therefore my orders are to take you back to your home. What you do after is up to you, but I warn you if you come back, the next time we will deliver you to the Illicitums."

Everything he said made sense, and they were right not to trust my people, especially after they gave up one of their own. Yet, I was still confused. Why did my faction tell them I was coming in the first place? That was the real question and the only one that needed answers.

"Why did your council member tell you to kill me?"

"He was just joking." Mydon chuckled. "We love theatrics."

"That wasn't a funny joke." I squinted, but he said nothing. His facial expression, however, told me that he *did* enjoy that weird joke.

Through the rest of the journey, I tried to ask him a few questions about his new council, but he didn't respond to any of them, speaking only when it was something general and unimportant. For a faction that hates mine to the core, he was surprisingly nice. He treated me decently and even laughed twice when I tried to joke myself out of boredom.

When we reached Lake Zuno, the grand lake that holds most of the islands of my faction, he brought the wood down to the water and floated it to the main city of Lunar. At the island, I stepped on the ground first. I looked around, contemplating what I would do next, but before my brain formulated any thoughts, I felt a needle's sting in my neck. I tried to turn around to look at him, but my legs were weak, and my eyelids grew heavy. I fought to keep them open but couldn't.

The last thing I saw was Mydon putting something on my forehead, then everything faded away as I felt my body crash against the ground.

MISPLACED SEEDS

When I woke up, I found myself inside a small cell with dark walls. The room had no windows other than a small one on the door that was locked shut by three metal bars. I instantly felt for my seeds, but none of them were there. My heartbeat tripled with that realization, and I jumped off the ground toward the door, pounding on it with all my strength, but my body felt weak. My breathing grew heavier with each knock, and my thoughts ran crazy as I realized I could no longer manipulate my body functions. Ever since I was born with my seeds like everyone in my faction, I trained on how to use them. Each seed controlled an aspect of my body, whether it was my inner organs or my mind. The seeds also allowed me to boost my abilities and do things that were impossible for other factions. I had never felt so weak before, and my worst fear had come true.

I imagined putting more power in my arms as I banged on the door but could hear the sound getting less powerful with every touch.

"Hello!" I shouted, but there was no response. "Anybody," I shouted again, but even my voice had lost some of its power. My tears rushed to my cheeks as I fell to the ground, feeling the connection between every limb in my body and my brain disappearing. Some time after, I lost awareness of my surroundings.

When I felt a foot hit my side, I woke up, struggling to look upward toward whoever stood by my side.

"Get up," a man ordered.

"My seeds," I said with a faint voice.

"I said, get up," the man shouted.

"I can't control my body. I need my seeds."

"It's been only a few hours since we took your seeds away. Your body is still at its full strength. Your fear is just making you think the worst has already happened." He kicked me again. "Now, get up."

As I heard his words, I focused on my strength and realized he was right. Within a few seconds, my brain was functioning again, and I regained control over my body. I had driven myself into weakness because I knew what losing the seeds meant, but at that moment, it was all a placebo. However, even though I was back to my full strength, I knew that I had to get my seeds at any cost or what I put myself into for a moment would become my reality.

I took consecutive deep breaths, focusing on my strength and rose to my feet before locking eyes with the protector who stood in military gear, his armor covering his entire body.

"Where are my seeds?" I asked with a calm tone.

He said nothing and grabbed my arm with force before handcuffing me. He then turned and stalked out of the cell, pulling me behind him.

"Where are you taking me?" I asked, but he didn't answer. We walked through several corridors, and when we reached another room, he uncuffed me and pushed me inside. I turned back toward him and tried to run to the door, but he had already locked it. This door, however, had no windows. I punched it and turned toward the other end of the room. This one was bigger with white walls and a large light falling off the ceiling. A table centered the room, and on its other side, I saw the director.

"Hello, Oran," he said with a regular tone, his face vacant of expressions.

"Boss!" With hasty steps, I took the seat opposite him. "What's going on?"

"You're the one who needs to tell me what's going on. Why did you infiltrate Kala?"

My head jerked back as my eyes narrowed. "You gave me this mission."

"That's not true."

"Yes, you did. It was in your office, and then you erased your memory after saying that I was on my own."

The director put one hand in his pocket, the other extended on the table between us, a finger tapping its surface. The blue seed atop his white forehead blinked. A moment later, he ran his fingers across his short black hair and shook his head.

"Even if that was true, which I don't believe since there is no reason for me to send you on such a mission, being caught would still be your fault."

"That's the thing. Someone sold me out and told the Kalangous I was coming. This mission was doomed to fail from the start. You need to tell who else knew about this mission."

The director laughed. "You are indeed the greatest of my spies." His face turned serious, a little gleam camping over his light-green eyes. "I didn't want to believe it when they told me you were working for Delphia, but you, of all people, should have remembered that we have cameras in all our rooms. Tell me, Oran, why did Matso tell you that you will meet him again right before he left."

"How in the name of the Lotus should I know? You know that Delphians are weird. Perhaps he foresaw it. You can't believe that I'm working for another faction just because one of them said something suspicious. This is how they manipulate the world around them," I said, my voice raised.

"If it was just simple words, I would have agreed with you, but you proved the informant to be right when you took a mission for them."

"For the hundredth time, *you* gave me that mission. You asked me to find the location of the Kalangous' gates."

"Keep your voice down," he said, locking his eyes with mine. "This entire conversation is a courtesy for the time we worked together and only because I wanted to see why you would betray your own people. We gave you everything you wanted and more." He took a deep breath. "Plus, I would never ask you to look for the magical gates. Our peace accords with the Illicitums prevent us from digging into the origin of Kala's magic. I would never risk betting my entire faction against the wrath of the palace."

I pushed the chair with force and rose to my feet, leaning toward him. "You manipulated me."

The director brushed his black seed, his armor crawling over his body and covering it, then he pulled out his gun and aimed it at me. "Sit down. You are in no position to behave like this."

I reached for my black seed on the top of my right arm, but when I remembered it wasn't there, I took back my seat, tears sliding down my cheeks. "By the Lotus, I swear, I'm not a double agent. You are the one who sent me there."

He closed his eyes while heaving a heavy sigh. "You need to change your narrative, Oran. If you stick with this story, I won't be able to help you."

"It's the truth," I said amidst my cries. "Please, just give me my seeds. I don't deserve this."

"I'm sorry, Oran, but there's nothing I can do about this. Not anymore." He stood, and I heard the door open at the same time. As the director reached my side, I tried to grab his arm while sobbing to beg for my seeds, but a protector had already stepped in, tackled me, and twisted my arm behind my back before cuffing it again. My boss glanced at me one more time, then stepped out of the room before the protector, covered in a uniform glowing blue at the shoulder, dragged me back to my cell.

THE SINS WE DON'T MAKE

As I sat in the corner of my cell, my back resting against the wall, I bit my lips until they bled to stop my crying. I had to tell myself that even though losing my seeds meant that I couldn't enhance any part of my body, I was still me. My brain and my training were still there, and even though my body would degrade over time, it would be months before I fully lose myself.

I jumped to my feet and started pacing the cell. I recalled the director's words about needing to change my narrative so he could help me but found it more important to understand what really happened. That was the key.

I closed my eyes and thought about who would benefit from me getting caught. There was no way only the director and I knew about this mission. He was right about one thing though, he wouldn't order such a dangerous mission by himself, but who else could know about it? The higher-ups? Even if I'm still the best spy in Lunar, it doesn't make sense that they would give me up, unless...

I rested my forehead against the door and breathed slowly, forcing myself to consider who would want to get rid of me.

When I opened my eyes again, I had an idea. While still by the door, I knocked on it calmly. "Is anyone there?"

In return, I heard a metal bar bang against the door from the other side.

"I don't want trouble," I said quietly. "Would you please tell the director that I'm ready to confess?"

The guard said nothing, but I heard footsteps moving away and believed he listened to me. I returned to the corner and reassumed my seat on the ground with my back against the wall, legs bent, elbows resting on my knees, and hands clasped together under my chin while my gaze focused on the door.

The guard disappeared for a long time, and I began to think that my plan had failed until I heard the lock open. I jumped to my feet and rushed to the door, my hands held together in front of me. The protector looked into my eyes and handcuffed me before pulling me through the corridors once more until we reached the white room. As the protector removed the cuffs, I turned to the chair where the director had been sitting the first time, and my grin widened.

"I should have known it would be you," I said, taking the seat opposite Nerva, my old partner. She met my gaze with an empty expression, her brown eyes steady, and her ear-length hair perfectly still.

"I have no idea what you are talking about. I was sent here to hear your confession," she said with a calm tone.

"Were these the director's order?"

She nodded without breaking our eye contact.

"Alright, here is what I came to confess. I did betray my faction—"

Nerva jumped with a violent move, banging her two hands against the table. "You will pay for this."

"However," I continued, my tone unchanged. "I didn't do it alone. I had a partner who facilitated my connection with Delphia."

Her eyes narrowed as she took back her seat. "Who?"

I smirked, "You."

Nerva laughed. "It's true then. Without your seeds, you go crazy first."

"It's the truth, and I would like to testify to it in court."

"No one will believe you."

"It's my word against yours."

"We have your seeds, Orantine. The protectors will pull out your memories and see that I had nothing to do with your claims."

"True, but they will also find no sign of my betrayal and will think that I erased my memories of you like I did with the Delphian ones."

Nerva interlocked her fingers and started tapping them against one another. "What do you want?" she asked after a moment of silence.

"My seeds back and my name cleared."

"That will be impossible."

I opened my mouth to speak, but she interrupted before I could utter a word.

"However, I may be able to help you secure a route out of the faction."

"This is what you wanted all along, Nerva. Isn't it? Me out of the picture so you could have a chance at being the best spy."

"I have already proved it. I put you exactly where I wanted you to be. Perhaps you can gain some time by claiming I was your accomplice, but if you want your seeds back, you will have to abandon this faction forever."

"And do what?"

"Delphia accepts asylum. Maybe, you will have better luck with them."

"I wasn't really their spy," I said, tears on the edge of my eyes.

"Doesn't mean they can't take you in, and if it didn't work, there's an entire world beyond our continent that you could explore."

I closed my eyes, a single tear escaping onto my cheeks. "My seeds?"

"You will have them back, I promise, but after you get out of the faction."

As I nodded in approval, Nerva stood and walked to the door before knocking on it. She turned to me just as it was opening. "If I were you, I wouldn't sleep tonight."

***

My eyes remained wide open despite how tired my body felt. It didn't matter that Nerva warned me to stay awake. My body was determined to do it anyway. As I sat in the darkness, I put my fist on my chest and started praying. "Oh, mighty Lotus, hear me. I would never betray you or those who carry your essence in their veins, but right now, I need your protection. Oh, mighty Lotus, look over me and guide me into your light."

My eyes followed the light of the corridor as the door opened. Nerva was standing there, her gaze focused on me. "Let's go," she said. "We don't have a lot of time."

I jumped to my feet and followed her. As we ran from one corridor to another, I saw the protectors on the ground. They appeared to be breathing, so I assumed they were only unconscious. Nerva led me to the fire exit, and through it, we climbed up to the surface. Outside, I took a deep breath to taste the fresh air before looking around me and realizing that we weren't inside any of the Lunardis cities. In fact, we were by the border, just behind Lake Zuno. The two of us ran through the trees edging my faction and Delphia's, stopping only after we crossed the unguarded borders.

"My seeds?" I asked the moment we halted.

Nerva pulled a rectangular-shaped box out of her pocket, and as I reached for it, she pulled it back, guarding it behind her body.

"I just have one question," she said. "How did you know it was me who sold you out?"

"I didn't. I would have used the same technique on whoever waited for me in the room, even if it was the director himself. However, the moment I saw you, I knew it couldn't have been anybody else."

"I see." She held the box out in my direction, and I quickly took it from her, opening it and releasing a sigh of relief as I saw my seeds.

She continued while I placed the seeds back on my body. "Remember, Oran, you can't go back to Lunar. Your escape just now has cemented the charges on you."

"I get it."

Without a goodbye, Nerva started to retrace her steps, but I called for her. "One day, I will come for you, Nerva, and when I do, I promise you that you will regret what you've done."

She smiled in a way that made me feel like she didn't care about my threat which irritated me. But we didn't exchange any more words as each of us moved in a different direction.

AN EYE ON THE FUTURE

Once I was far enough from the borders of my faction, I stopped and felt for my seeds again, then focused on my inner veins and sensed how my blood moved between my heart and my seeds. My heart slowly calmed as each of my seeds blinked when I focused on it. Only then did the fatigue from being awake for nearly a full day hit me. My eyelids grew heavy, and I laid on the forest ground, allowing myself to get the sleep I needed.

When I woke up, I removed my yellow seed and pulled my pod out to ride it. I spent the whole day on my lotus pod, moving between Delphia's outer forests until I reached their capital. When I entered the city, my heart began to race again, and my red seed started blinking. As I flew between their high glass towers, I found the streets empty of people. I thought perhaps it was calm because it was nearly night time, so I found a corner and set up camp. But when the morning came again, there was still no one.

I roamed the streets of a city filled with skyscrapers and no sign of life. What I also found weird was that there wasn't a single entrance. I couldn't go inside any building. After a few hours of walking in a dead city, I took out my lotus pod again and used it to reach the top of one of the skyscrapers, and that was when I saw it. The whole city lived on the rooftops. Even the roads were up there. From above, I saw a world different from ours. Delphia was the only other faction in the continent of Mastoperia with technology and a life that appeared quite close to ours. However, their faces were different, more serious. Everyone I saw wore the same thing, a white suit made of silk, wide enough to run in. Only their collars differed in colors.

Everyone looked at me as I stepped off my pod onto one of the rooftops, but no one spoke. The way their eyes followed me made me feel judged as if everyone but me knew what was going to happen to me.

I was sure that someone would approach me eventually. After all, this was a faction where people knew the future. Surely, they figured out why I was there, the same way Matso said we would meet again.

I stood in place for half an hour until two Delphians finally came to talk to me. They had red collars and carried swords, but I didn't feel threatened by them.

"Are you here to seek asylum?" asked one of the two.

"I am," I said, surprised by the depth of what he saw. Not only did he pinpoint my location in a large city, but he knew exactly why I was there, and I couldn't help but wonder what else he knew.

"Follow me," he said.

At first, when I saw them move on foot, I thought we would walk to wherever they were taking me, but then I had to pull out my lotus pod again to keep up with them as they ran across the rooftops. They were clearly skilled in the art of parkour and didn't seem bothered by the distance or the speed. For them, it was simply a brisk walk. For me, it was sport.

Through the roof entrance of another building, they took me to an office and asked me to wait. It took four hours for someone to call my name, which annoyed me because there was no one else in the waiting area, but I had no other choice.

Eventually, I joined an investigator in another room, and he asked me why I sought asylum. I knew I wouldn't be able to fool him, so I told him everything that happened. I told him about how I infiltrated Kala, and how my faction handed me to them, then how they imprisoned me and took away my seeds. The investigator had many questions, and I answered them all, never once arousing suspicion. Why would I when I was telling the truth? At the end of the meeting, the investigator said he empathized with my story and that I passed the first step, but there was an orientation I had to go through to see if I would be accepted or not.

The orientation wasn't on the same day, so he gave me a nice room to sleep in for the night. The room had an entire wall turned into a glass window that overlooked other skyscrapers. I pulled a chair to the window and watched the moon that night, my gaze following its light as it reflected on the glass towers, disappearing only against the different lights of some other rooms in the distance. From my view, the city looked a lot more alive even when I saw no one, which felt strange considering how the faction looked dead from below.

The morning after, I walked to the orientation room, and to my surprise, it was someone that I had already met, Matso, the man I saw at the meeting with the director before all my trouble started.

The room had simple dark-green walls with several student-like desks and a neon light attached to the ceiling. Matso leaned against a desk at the front of the room, his hands clutching the wooden edge.

"Miss Orantine. I told you we would meet again." He had a big smile on his face.

"So...You knew." I pressed on my teeth. "You knew what was going to happen to me."

"Once again, I can see the future, and perhaps you need to get used to it. You are asking for asylum in a faction where everyone has this power."

"I thought you could only see your own future, nothing more."

"Meeting you again was part of my future, and so is the conversation we are having right now."

"I guess there's no need for me to speak then since you already know what I will say."

"I do know, but the conversation still needs to happen. Otherwise, we would never talk to one another."

I agreed with his logic but still preferred to change the subject. "I thought you were the head of the correspondence office. Is orientation part of your job too?"

"Not really, but when I heard it was you, I asked to be the one who gives you all the details."

"Why?" I drew my brows together.

"Because I'm interested in your story."

I sighed as I sat in the first desk chair opposite him. "I thought this was an orientation. I already explained my story yesterday."

"You're right, again. I'm here to tell you about what you can and cannot do as long as you're here and to see if you will accept it and pledge by its rules." He paused, and the corners of his eyes lifted. "But maybe you could tell me your story over dinner later?"

I knew he was asking me out, but I didn't feel interested, so I changed the subject. "Does this mean I'm in already?"

"Why would you think so? Right," he said with a chuckle, "because I asked you out. Well, I do feel that you will pass the orientation, but even if you don't, you would still have the chance to appeal, and that would give you a few days in Delphia." His lips widened. "We could use the time to bond and get to know one another."

I wanted to grunt at him for not getting the hint, but I had to appear polite. I needed to be admitted into Delphia. "I would like to see how everything goes with my request first," I said.

"Of course." He pulled out a chair and positioned himself opposite me. "I shall begin the orientation then."

I nodded, waiting for him to start.

"As a refugee in Delphia, you cannot live inside any of the cities. We will give you a map of the locations where you can set up your house, and you can choose one. However, no one will help you with the build. Is that okay?"

"Yes." I blinked in approval.

"You can never leave the faction without permission. If you wish to leave at any time, you can request a departure slip from the office of refugees. If approved, your asylum will be revoked, and you won't be allowed to return to Delphia again."

"Why?" My eyes widened. "I understand that I can't go back to Lunar, but what if I want to visit any of the other two factions, Kala or Averett."

"You can't. Delphia is the only faction that accepts asylum requests. We do that because we believe in others' right to live and believe that a misunderstanding with your own faction shouldn't be the end of the world. Once we accept your application, you will be under our protection. If Lunar asks that we hand you over, we will refuse and then must deal with the consequences."

He took a deep breath. "I know you were a spy, and you used to sneak into other factions, but you have to forget about that. If you stay here, you will no longer be a spy. When regular people travel to other factions, they go through an application process that rarely gets accepted, so, in reality, no one really travels outside of their faction. Plus, we wouldn't be able to protect you if you were outside Delphia. This is the second condition. Do you accept it?"

I sighed, hating the idea, but he was right, and I had to think of myself as a regular citizen, "I accept."

The corners of his eyes lifted again. "You will receive a six-month integration period, through which you can build your house. During that time, the government will pay you a monthly salary equal to the minimum wage. Don't worry, it will be enough. Once the six months are over, the government will offer you five positions in community service, which we believe fit your skills. You must choose one of the five. If you refuse, your asylum will be canceled."

"What kind of jobs?" I raised my brows.

"I don't know. You will go through an evaluation to determine what's best for you. Do you accept?"

"Yes."

"Until you finish your house and for no more than six months, you will stay in the same room you had last night. After that, you won't be allowed inside any of the cities for more than two nights a month. Breaking that rule will give you a strike. If you receive three strikes, your asylum will be canceled. Do you accept?"

"Yes."

"You can mingle with other Delphians. They can be your friends, and you can marry a Delphian, but you can never have children. If you do, your baby will be taken away, and we will kick you out. If you try to escape with the child, we will hunt and kill you. Do you accept?"

I looked at Matso in silence. This was the first time he averted his eyes away from me. I could see he was uncomfortable with this condition. I wasn't comfortable with it either. I didn't think I would have children right away, but to live knowing that I could never have one was a big decision.

He didn't try to rush an answer out of me, which I appreciated. "I will go get myself a glass of water. Would you like one too?" he asked.

I nodded. I did need water to swallow what he said. I felt trapped between two choices. Either go back to my faction and die or live in Delphia for the rest of my life, knowing that my legacy would end with me. I weighed both options against each other. I was a spy, and I knew how to make tough decisions. I needed to worry about the now and leave the future for later.

When he returned, as he put the glass of water on my desk, I asked, "Why can't I have children?"

He heaved a heavy sigh. "This faction strives on the power of seeing the future and the loyalty of its citizens. If you were to have children with a Delphian, their genes wouldn't be pure. They could have the power of both factions or develop something new that we haven't seen before. This could be dangerous to everyone, especially if they decide to start their own group. No one is willing to accept this, and all Mastoperia will seek to eliminate them. We would rather you have no children than find ourselves in a position where we need to kill them. The truth is the glue holding our world together is not that strong."

"Has it happened before?"

"In the thousand years since there were four factions?" He nodded. "Many times. Regardless of the separation between the factions and the number of wars, people still find a way to love each other. But the children always suffered. Most of the time, they were incomplete and suffered more problems than they had powers, and in the times when it was promising, we killed them."

"Have you ever thought that maybe the answer to our world was that we become one? If we all shared the same powers, there would be no difference."

"The concept is beautiful, and I respect it, but it would be the case if all the new children had the same power. What will most likely happen is that we will have new and different sets of abilities. Instead of four factions, we could end up with ten or twenty, and then it will become much more dramatic. Trust me."

"You seem to know a lot about this."

"Part of my job is to know a little about everything."

I wasn't convinced, though. Matso sounded like someone who had researched the subject well. I would understand it if orientation was his job. He would have needed to know more about their conditions, but he already said that he only volunteered because it was me. His face also lacked any signs of emotions this whole time, even though he was smiling easily before.

"Do you accept?" he asked.

"Yes."

I noticed his brows rise at my answer, but he quickly hid his reaction with a nod.

"The last condition is that you cannot show any of your religious or spiritual beliefs in public. You cannot have any other person follow any of those beliefs either. You can practice anything you want inside your own home, and only your home. Do you accept?"

"I do." This one I understood, and it didn't matter anyway. To worship the Lotus like I do, you would have to have the seeds or, at the very least, the lotus genes. None of them would understand, and I wasn't in the business of fanatics.

"All right then." He stood. "I hereby pronounce that we accept your application. This conversation was recorded, and you can request it in any future hearings."

He extended his hand to me. "Welcome to Delphia, Miss Orantine."

"Thank you." I shook his hand, my face empty of any expression. "What should I do now?"

"You are free to go back to your room and rest, and in two days, you will receive a call to go check the locations where you can begin to build your house. They will also give you all the papers you need." He smiled, taking a step closer to me. "Unless you want to join me for dinner later."

"Maybe another time." I faked a smile. "I'm tired and do need the rest you offered." I turned around and moved away before he asked me out one more time.

THE HOUSE OF SAITERS

When I returned to my room that night, I laid on the bed, my body sinking into the large mattress, my arms spread across the bed at the level of my shoulders, yet neither of my fingers had reached the edge of the mattress. I brushed my black seed, and my clothes retreated into my body, leaving me naked, and allowing my skin to enjoy the touch of the silk sheets.

I stared out at the multiple colors lighting the skyscrapers across from my chamber and wondered if this was it. Was this going to be my life from now on? Should I let go of my faction and forget about the truth? Could I really live a simple life, an ordinary one where I'm confined within the borders of one faction? Questions swirled in my mind, one after the other, until I drifted into sleep.

When the sun began to shine upon the world again, its light reflected on the glass towers then onto my face, waking me. I rubbed my eyes and rolled away from the direct light, but my body had decided it had enough sleep, so I dragged myself out of bed and into the shower.

When I came out of the bathroom, I stood in front of the mirror and looked at my pale skin. At first, I brushed my black seed and thought about my daily outfit as the metal in my blood crawled out to the top of my skin, transforming into leather-like material and covering my entire body in my regular blue suit. My lips pursed into a fine line as I saw my reflection in the mirror. I thought perhaps, it would be better if Delphians saw me trying to fit in. So I brushed the same seed one more time and watched as my tight suit turned into a wide one, its color changing to white like everyone else in Delphia, and its material imitating the look of silk. When it was time for my collar to change, I wasn't sure which color to choose, but after playing with different colors, I opted to make it blue, my faction's official color. With sneakers on my feet, I walked out of the room and climbed to the roof to leave the building.

I walked from one rooftop to the other, using the countless bridges they built to connect their buildings with one another. The day was young, yet life had already resumed its natural order. While I marched, Delphians ignored my existence as they free ran everywhere. I even saw groups of children performing flips from one bridge to the other rather than taking the long road around. It was refreshing to see them use their sport for daily commute, rather than ignore the health of their body and depend on their technology like my faction members were now doing. However, the rooftops and bridges all carried the same dull gray coating, with colors visible only in the shops scattered atop the buildings. They had a multitude of commercial entities, but libraries were the dominating business, with at least one atop every building. After passing several of them, I became curious about the type of books they offered, so I walked into one. Once I stepped inside, the shopkeeper greeted me with a smile. He wore their standard clothes with a white collar atop his suit.

"Welcome," he said with a smile and presented his hand for a shake. When I met the shake, he cradled my hand and paused for a second, his face turning vacant of expressions. "I see," he said, his grin returning. "We have a variety of books, but..." He pulled his hand back and walked away. With my eyebrows drawn together, I froze in place, unsure what he was talking about, but he quickly returned with a book.

"This is a murder mystery novel that I'm sure you will like," the shopkeeper said, handing me a pocketbook with a character holding a magnifying glass on the cover."

"How did you...? Right." I smiled. "You looked into the future."

He nodded. "Reading is the best activity to indulge yourself in, but it can become daunting if you find yourself stuck with the wrong book. I wouldn't want you to give up something so enthralling, just because you don't know your own taste."

I looked at the book in my hand and met the seller's eyes again. "I appreciate you helping me, but I can't—"

"Don't worry about the payment. This one is free, and when the authorities pay you, you are welcome to pay for the next in the series."

"How do you know that I will want to read the next one?"

His grin widened again.

"Of course," I said with a smile and took the book, thanking him before I walked back into the street. As I continued to march across the capital, I started to feel the heat of the sun against my skin and understood why they all dressed in white. I looked up at the clear sky one more time, then walked to the edge of the building I was on top of. I wanted to see how their lower world looked from up there, and that was when I realized that we were high enough that even the clouds couldn't rise all the way to the top.

Delphia was certainly fascinating, and the more I saw of it, the more I wanted to know about this faction. Delphia and Lunar are allies, and we had been for centuries. Therefore, there was never a reason for me to do a job on their land. But then I thought of how it wouldn't be possible. No spy, no matter how good they are, would be able to fool a faction that can accurately predict what will happen long before it comes to pass. Perhaps, that was why my faction insisted on them being our allies.

After a while, I started to hear the hunger sing in my stomach, so I pulled out my pod and flew back to my building. When I reached my room, I found a meal waiting for me outside, and I smiled at how the Delphians thought of everything.

I took the food into my room and placed it on the mahogany table by the window. I ate slowly because even though the food was delicious, I caught myself drifting away and remembering the times

Bodya cooked for me. I cursed myself for thinking about him again, and how after five and half years of our breakup, his image in my mind was as fresh as when we separated from one another. Even my heart ached with the same level of pain.

To ease my misery, I pressed the red seed above the location of my heart with force until my brain was thinking more about physical pain than it did heartbreak, a trick that I learned growing up to protect myself against emotional suffering.

However, escaping thoughts of Bodya meant that I was once again thinking about my faction and what Nerva forced me to do. Stuck between my mind and heart, I took both the blue and red seeds out of my body, allowing myself a moment to calm down and ignore my reality. Sleep was the other friend I could count on that night.

***

The day after, I went back to the asylum office, where they showed me a map of Delphia with markings of several locations within their small forests and the western desert. I chose to live in the forest, edging my faction and theirs, knowing that deep inside, it was because I wanted to be as close to home as possible, even though I would still be living nearly a thousand miles away from my faction.

The official also gave me a magnetic card that he said I could use to pay for my needs, but he didn't need to explain that part since it looked identical to the voin cards we used in Lunar. Perhaps, it was us who gave them the technology. At the end of the meeting, he gave me a handwritten invitation from Matso to meet him for dinner, but I politely declined and told him to inform Matso that I'd rather be alone, at least for now. Whether Matso knew that what he said to me back in Lunar would influence my capture or not didn't matter. He was still partly the reason for what transpired in my life, and I didn't want to deal with him.

When I left the office, I rode my pod and flew to where my new home would be, but as I descended through the trees, I saw him. Matso was waiting for me, and my immediate reaction was a head shake and a silent grunt. When I put my feet on the ground, however, I forced a smile as our eyes met.

"What are you doing here?" I asked through my teeth.

"I wanted to see if you would like the spot you chose to build your home in."

"I have only just chosen it, and you weren't there. You can't tell me that this too was part of your own future."

Matso adjusted his brown collar. "There are a lot of ways to manipulate our powers and see things that don't directly affect us. Once again, you need to get used to it, or your life here will be pointlessly difficult."

"Alright, alright," I said, rolling my eyes before darting my gaze around. "Well... I like it if that will make you happy."

"I'm happy when you are. The question is, why don't you like me? What did I do to you?"

I sighed now that everything was on the table. "Can't you saite or look into the future or whatever it is you do to see what's wrong?"

"I can only see actual events, not emotions, and unless you plan to say what's wrong, then I can't foresee it, no matter how many versions of the future I examine."

Nodding, I turned away again and continued to study the location, hoping that he would see that I wanted him to leave. Yet, it didn't work.

Matso came to my side and started imitating my inspection. "How do you plan to build your house?" he asked.

"I don't know yet, but I'm sure I can use my seeds to find a recording or a tutorial about how to build a house by hand. I will teach myself."

"How about I do it for you?"

I chuckled. "Are you a builder now too? Plus, I thought your faction's rule was that I build my own house."

"No, they simply indicate that the faction itself won't help you with the build, but if I was to personally hire contractors and pay for them myself, it wouldn't be against the rules."

"Thank you, but I don't need you to pay for me. I can take care of myself."

"I'm sure you can, but I didn't say you wouldn't be required to pay me back. Once the faction assigns you with a job, you will be able to quickly refund me, and I will expect every transaction out of my account returned."

"Once again—"

"Think about it like this," he interrupted. "With me paying, you can have a house that resembles those in your faction. After all, I would have to hire Lunardis contractors."

"Why? You don't have your own?"

He laughed. "Miss Orantine, we don't build anything. Your people do it for us."

"That sounds strange."

"That's just the way the world works. We design, and you construct."

I nodded. Part of me wanted to continue refusing his offer, but the idea of having a piece of my faction around me calmed my heart, so I accepted. I should have, of course, known that this agreement meant I would see Matso more often.

THE ONES WE REMEMBER

The first three months in Delphia passed faster than I thought they would. Delphians were more welcoming than I expected, and I found it interesting how they helped me uncover my real taste in so many small activities. I was discovering myself anew and gravitating toward falling in love with their culture. Yet, what fascinated me the most, was learning that the directors of their university were also the leaders of the faction. Two hundred and fifty professors ruled over Delphia from what they called the Skeptic Room, a fitting name for people who believe in theory more than application. Though, I would have just called them philosophers.

Three months was how long it took for my house to be ready. A few days before it was time to move in, Matso learned that he would be leaving for a weeklong job in another Delphian city. Anxious to see my new place, I asked him to saite the future and see if it was safe for me to pick up the keys from the Lunardis contractors myself.

With his confirmation, I woke up with an elevated heartbeat and a blinking red seed on the promised day, but I didn't care how my body felt. I covered my skin with my regular Lunardis leather outfit and rode my pod to the outer forest.

I shivered the moment my eyes fell on my new home. It was perfect. A two-story building with a Lotus-shaped roof, its decorative petals alternating between the six colors of my seeds. From outside, the top of the walls carried an intricate art of large leaves and interconnected vines painted atop a gray that matched my faction's Lake Zuno. My gaze remained glued to the house even as I put my feet on the ground and retracted the pod into my yellow seed. Tears flowed down my cheeks. It was perfect, but it wasn't Lunar. Yet, I knew this was as close as I could get, so I wiped my tears away and replaced them with a smile before strolling through my new front garden.

A variety of plants formed a circle on the ground with five sunflowers at the center, all following the sun in harmony. My brows raised at the sunflowers for a moment because I didn't remember telling Matso it was my favorite flower, but then I remembered that I didn't need to tell him at all.

As I walked closer to the entrance and began to hear the chatter coming from inside, my heart skipped another beat, and my feet began to move with caution, but all the fear went away once I popped my head through the door, and my eyes fell on the living room with its vivid blue walls and the glass dining table with a base that matched the chandelier and metal chairs.

Every item was true to my taste and in the exact place where I would put it. And thank the lotus, there was a lot of my faction's technology. Some of which was still being installed, and that was when I finally noticed my people putting the final touches on my house.

They didn't pay attention to me, though, not even when I thanked them for their hard work, which I didn't find strange. Lunardis know they do a great job every time and wait for no praise.

After giving myself a tour, I walked out of the house to see its final addition. I was happy in my mind until a voice brought me back to reality.

"Orantine?"

I heard my name as I turned a corner to reach the back garden, and my heart raced. At first, it was because I believed I recognized the voice, but then I started to sweat when my brain thought of the worst. The stranger didn't call for me in a threatening tone, but the fact that whoever it was recognized who I am scared me. My fingers shook as I slowly turned around.

"It's me, Bodya. Don't you remember me?"

When I saw him, and even before he had spoken, my heartbeat jumped to an even faster rhythm. And with my first thought confirmed, my legs weakened. Of course, I remembered him. How could I forget the love of my life? If only he knew how prevalent in my thoughts he was. I would have changed my whole life for him, but five years before, he decided to act like a prick and broke up with me because he thought that me joining the protector's academy would break us apart. It wouldn't have, but his stupid stubbornness is what did it.

I took a deep breath to control my emotions and faked a smile, or maybe it was genuine, I'm not sure.

Bodya's grin widened. "I didn't know you were in the real estate market now. What happened to being a protector?

"Nothing happened." I lifted my shoulders. "I saw it through."

"Then why are you here?" He raised his brows.

I quickly examined several answers before finding a lie that would make him feel I was better than him. "This house is mine." I took a step toward him. "I'm moving here as a diplomat to facilitate communications between our faction and Delphia."

"We have diplomats now? I thought they were only assigned to the Forbidden Palace."

"It's a new thing." I forced another smile. "I'm the first."

"Look at you." He gently punched my arm with a light expression. "You're making history. I knew you could do it."

I held my breath to control my feelings. I didn't want my red seed to blink due to the mess in my emotions and give him a clue of how I felt. I wanted to tell him I missed him and ask if he had someone in his life, but I couldn't. It was too late. Still, I was boiling from within, wondering how he could be at such ease around me.

Once again, I used my training to suppress my emotions and appear neutral. "So, you are a contractor now? I thought you wanted to be a scientist."

"No, no. I'm a scientist." He shook his head. "We installed a brand-new invention in the house, and I'm here to supervise it."

"Yeah." I smiled. "What does it do?"

"Wait." He pulled a rectangular-shaped box from his pocket then removed a piece of glass that looked like a small seed. "This allows you to control the entire house from the comfort of your seeds."

I raised my brows high.

"Here." He handed me the seed. "Put it on your blue seed and think about the outdoor lights. And don't worry, they are magnetic and will stick on their own."

I did as he asked, but nothing happened. "It's not working."

"Huh." He opened his mouth. "Try again, please."

I shook my head. "Nothing is happening."

"I see." He lowered his chin. "I'm sorry about that. It's a new invention, so it needs some tweaking."

"It's okay." I waved my shoulders in a quick move.

"Tell you what, you keep them with you," he said, handing me the box containing four more identical glass seeds, "and I will research the one not working." He removed the one I had placed on my forehead. "Once I fix the issue, I will contact you and update them remotely."

"So, I can't use the other ones either?"

"Please don't." His eyes bulged. "I don't want there to be any problems while I'm away. Once I fix them, I will tell you, and then you can give it another shot."

"Okay. Why is there more than one, though?"

"Spare parts in case you lose any."

"Smart. Though it looks like one is missing. The box has a place for six glass seeds, but there are only four here. Counting the one you have, where did the last one go? You are not going to try and take control of my house, are you?" I asked with an uncomfortable chuckle.

"Who knows, maybe I will." He winked at me before his face turned serious again. "I just picked a standard storage box rather than create a special one. Anyway, my job here is done."

He shook my hand and called for the others to leave. "Good luck with your job, Miss Diplomat." He smiled again before his crew came out one by one. When the last Lunardis stepped out of my house, she handed me the keys without uttering a word as if she already knew it was for me. In fact, none said a word to me. They just pulled out their lotus pods, rode them, and flew away as if I wasn't there. Only Bodya gave me a wave goodbye.

My eyes followed him as he disappeared through the trees, and I took a deep breath. Following the encounter, I was sure my emotions would be in turmoil for a while. I decided to take a nap so my body could have time to breathe again. However, I couldn't sleep, even after laying on my new bed. Yet the issue wasn't my bed. It was the fact that each time I closed my eyes, I started to see strange images. Images that my brain translated into memories even though I had no recollection of them.

THE POWER OF THE MIND

The first thing I saw in my mind as I laid on my new bed was Bodya. His face was identical to how it looked when I saw him earlier in the garden and not of the eighteen-year-old Bodya I dated. Yet we were looking into each other's eyes with passion, and I could feel how our fingers interlocked. Darting my gaze around, I became even more immersed in my surroundings as my mind's image felt more like reality. We were walking through a building with lotus-inspired designs, but I didn't recognize the place, especially with all the retro-like devices scattered around.

"What do you think?" he asked with a chuckle.

"Looks old. Older than you even." I stuck my tongue out before immediately feeling a shiver inside my skin that didn't make it to the outside of my body. Speaking words that I had no intention to say brought back the realization that I was inside my mind and not actually there. I wasn't sure if I was daydreaming or already asleep, but not being able to bring myself back to reality enforced my belief in the latter.

"You know," Bodya said, pulling me back into the world my brain created, "we are the only faction that has the ability to experience everything more than once for the first time."

"What is that supposed to mean?" My eyes widened as I grabbed his arm, bringing him to a stop. "Was I here before?"

"Hey, Oran, nice to see you again."

I quickly turned toward the origin of the voice, but as my head moved, so did everything else. My surroundings faded away like paint peeling off a canvas and revealing completely new artwork. My body moved on its own as well, forcing me to fall into a glass chair at the center of a glass office with Bodya now sitting behind a desk between the two of us rather than standing by my side, and he was talking as if we were already in the middle of a conversation.

"Collars are their ranking system. With each advancement into the future, meaning how far they can see into the future, they also advance to a different color of collar. The average Delphian wears a white collar, for instance. Blue is for those who can see up to three years, red is for five years, brown is for a decade, and black is for a century or more. Brown is actually rare, and black is hardly ever witnessed."

"Now that you mentioned it, I think Matso wore a brown collar." I sighed. Yet again, that was not the reaction I wanted to give. Instead, I wondered why we were talking about Matso. This time, I tried to force myself to speak my thoughts, but before I could, Bodya's face started glitching, its features changing while my surroundings began to change again with the glass walls falling like wet paint dripping, revealing another wooden wall with a dark brown color that matched the new office appearing between Bodya and me. Only now, it was my old director behind the desk, and he threw a green file in front of me. My body moved on its own as I picked the file. Opening it, I found a single piece of paper with handwritten information on the top.

Name: Matso
Age: Twenty-four

"There's basically nothing here," I said.

"Exactly." He narrowed his eyes. "The smallest file we have on someone is one hundred filled pages."

"Do you think they are hiding something?"

"Either that or they don't know anything." He started to fidget with one of his gold pens on the desk. "Your mission is to know everything about Matso, and I mean *everything*."

I opened my mouth to speak, but again, my surroundings melted away, and I fell into a beach. This time, I was running in the sunshine, my body covered in a swimsuit that I fabricated with my purple seed. I turned back to see Bodya chasing me with a wide grin. I had the feeling that I wanted to put more force in my legs but was worried about something.

"Okay, okay," he shouted from a distance. "I give up."

Halting, I turned to him with a laugh and waited as he marched in my direction.

"You shouldn't run this fast, not for the next few months at least," he said and put his palm on my stomach.

***

Jumping upward with a quick move, I was back in my new bed with my eyes wide open. I wiped away the heavy sweat covering my skin and stepped to the ground before running outside the house, coming to a stop when I was in the middle of my garden. I wondered about what happened. It was clear that seeing Bodya had once again messed me up, but the images I saw felt so real, and I wondered if my mind was playing tricks on me. Could it be a side effect for temporarily losing my seeds when the protectors took them away? I couldn't tell why these images came to my mind, but as I thought about it, one thing became clear. I was missing Bodya while simultaneously worrying about what my faction did to me.

Considering the latest changes in my life and the sheer amount of information my brain acquired about Delphia in the last few months, I became convinced that my mind was combining everything together while organizing it in a way I would understand. That was why I saw Bodya in his scientist habitat after he told me that he became one, and it was he who put together everything I knew about Delphians.

Little by little, it was all making sense, but then there was Matso. Why did I see that green file about him?

I realized at that moment that despite hanging out with him multiple times over the last three months, what I read on the piece of paper in my mind's fabricated images was all I knew about him, and I began to wonder who was the real Matso as the thought of investigating him took over my mind.

PART THREE

Invisible Tracks

LIFE WITH PURPOSE

When Matso returned from his mission, I invited him for a meal in my new house. Partly because I wanted to thank him for everything he had done for me since I arrived in Delphia. However, I also had a hidden motive to learn more about him, so I could silence all the questions that swamped me.

As I expected, my invitation thrilled him. After all, this was a man who asked me out at least once whenever we met.

When he rang the bell on the planned evening, I brushed my purple seed and clicked my heels together to change my clothes into something nice. I chose a short blue halter dress that left my shoulders and half of my back exposed.

"You look beautiful," Matso said with a grin as soon as I opened the door.

"Thank you," I answered with a smile before inviting him inside.

"The house came together nicely." He turned in a circle, looking at everything.

"Thanks to you." I paused. "Would you like a tour?"

"Please."

I showed him around the house, and he commented on how I had more comfort than most Delphians. After the tour, we sat at the square metal table with a glass top in my living room, and I began serving dinner.

"So, is this a date?" he asked after telling me several times how the food looked and smelled good.

"It's a thank you." I saw the disappointment on his face, and I needed him to feel comfortable with me, so he would open his heart. "But if you play your cards right, it may be." His smile returned.

"I'm just happy to have you in my company."

"Why?" I couldn't help but ask. "Don't get me wrong. I like that you want to spend time with me, but I don't get why."

"Why not?" He shrugged.

"Because I'm from a different faction. I betrayed my own people and escaped like a coward, and now I live like a prisoner on your land."

"Is this how you feel? Like a prisoner?"

"Maybe not now, but at some point, it will feel like that. I will miss my people and realize that I can't see them whenever I want. Plus, my family must see me as a traitor. And don't forget that I can't decide the important things for myself anymore."

He sighed. "I'm sorry."

"It's not your fault. You're actually making this a lot easier for me."

"Still, sometimes I wish the world was different and that there were no borders and differences."

"Well, it's the reality we live in." The conversation was taking a sad turn, and I had to change the focus back on us, so he would feel more at ease with me. "You still didn't tell me what you like about me." I could see him blush, but I waited for him to answer. Verbalizing his feelings would help him feel closer to me, which would make my job easier.

"Did you know that Delphians have powers other than seeing the future?"

My eyes widened for a second, but I quickly blocked my emotions, forcing myself to appear calm. "No, I didn't. What kind of power?"

"It's nothing in particular, but every now and then, a Delphian will develop a power unique only to them. It's actually rare, and we haven't been able to find enough data to determine why it happens or from where it comes."

I knew that last part was a lie when he broke eye contact with me and focused his gaze on the table, but that was okay. I didn't expect him to tell me about such a secret on my first try, and I had time to find out more.

"So, what's yours?" I smiled and played with my hair to make him believe that his words were bringing me closer to him.

"I didn't say I had any."

I gave him what I hoped was a coy look but kept my stare unbroken.

"You're too smart for your own good, Orantine."

"Oran. You can call me Oran."

"Okay, Oran." He closed his eyes for a second, and I could tell his brain was savoring the moment and saving it in his happy box. My plan was working. "My power is that I can read people's minds."

I felt my heart jump out of my chest the same moment my back hit the back of my chair.

"Relax, it's not that simple."

"Can you read my mind right now?"

"No. Do you think if I could read your mind, I would have asked you tens of times to go out with me?"

"I don't think that would have stopped you. Even without that power, you could have still saited the future and saw my answer, but you didn't."

"I don't look into the future with you." His tone calmed. "Not when it comes to you and me. I want to experience things as they come."

I got the impression that he liked me more than I thought, but his secondary power still scared me, and it didn't seem as though he was lying about it.

"Tell me more about your power then." I put my spoon back on the empty plate and rested my arm on the table, leaning closer to him.

"I can't read everyone's mind. Only those I don't know. The closer you become to me, the less I can read."

"Is it psychological, or is this how your power works?"

"I don't know to be honest. I can usually see a colored halo around people. Those I don't know at all are yellow. Colleagues and acquaintances are orange. Friends and family are green. I can read every thought, even those hidden in the subconscious, if the color is yellow. If it's orange, I can only see immediate thoughts, and with green, I only get splashes that I can't control. Hearing the thoughts of family and friends is not my choice." He paused, twisting his mouth to the side. "And then there's you."

"What about me?"

"Your halo is a color I have never seen before. It's gray."

"That's a sad color." I faked a frown. "So, what does it mean?"

"Obviously, it means that I can read none of your thoughts and believe me, it's not for lack of trying."

I didn't feel good about his last statement, but I understood him. If I had this power, I would try to read everyone's thoughts, especially members of other factions. I would also try harder if I found only one person whose mind I couldn't read. Still, I felt invaded, as if he was trying to see me naked.

"What is your conclusion then? Why do *you* think you can't read my thoughts?" I had to appear casual about everything.

"I'm not sure you would like the answer."

"I can't judge until I hear it."

"Since the more I know the person, the less I can read their thoughts, I think, and this is only a theory, that we are meant for one another."

"Like fate?"

He nodded.

"Interesting theory," I said, keeping my face expressionless. I knew he was serious about not being able to read my mind because if he could, he would have known that I wasn't interested in him in a romantic way at all, but he was lucky because I needed to play this game until I knew everything about him.

I changed the subject after that and turned the evening into a more casual conversation. It didn't matter that he couldn't read my mind. If I pushed too much for information, he would become suspicious. He wasn't stupid.

When it got late, I told him I was tired and needed to wake up early the next day. He was understanding and moved directly toward the door without prolonging any conversation.

At the door, I could tell he was debating whether to lean in for a kiss or stick with a handshake, so I gave him my hand first to help him decide, then quickly put my other hand on top of his. A two-hand cradle would send him a signal that I enjoyed the evening and may look for more. It was all part of a manipulation technique I learned at the academy.

"Would it be okay if I invited you to dinner the next time? A Delphian restaurant, maybe?" He smiled, but I could see a slight blush tint his cheeks.

"Name the time and place, and I will be there." I patted his hand a couple of times before letting go.

His grin widened as he moved away. After I closed the door, I snuck a look through my peephole. He looked back at the house several times before disappearing into the forest, and that was how I knew that my plan would work, and I would soon know everything about him.

BREAKING BREAD

Three days later, I met Matso by the entrance of a restaurant that appeared classier than I expected. Golden decorations highlighted the green walls. Small tables for two with rose-colored tablecloths spread in a square pattern around a center bar. Bronze-framed chairs matched the color of a chandelier centering each table with three scented candles on top. Yet the prevalent odor was that of the food, and it was so good, my mouth watered in an instant.

The restaurant was large and nearly full, yet quiet as if there was no one there but us. I asked Matso about it, and he said they were using sound barriers, electrons that made sure the sound didn't reach more than one meter beyond each table in all directions. I looked down at the floor and saw a dark green frame surrounding each table with several tiny holes in it, and realized that must be how they released the electrons in a controlled field. As I darted my gaze around to savor the elegance, I noticed how the tables had only couples. I wanted to roll my eyes but feared Matso would see.

"The restaurant looks nice. I like it." I forced a smile as we took our seats.

"I'm glad you like it." Matso carried a genuine grin. "I always wanted to come here, but it's only for couples."

I looked at him with a frozen stare, pretending I had just realized his revelation and was confused by it.

He raised his palms as if to take back his words. "I don't mean that *we* are a couple. I just thought this would be a good opportunity to see the place from the inside."

I chuckled, partly to put him back at ease before he freaked out and shut down, and partly because I honestly felt amused by his reaction.

"Don't worry about it." I said with a small smile. "The place is lovely."

He released a quick sigh, and his shoulders relaxed. I could sense that he was calming down, but I needed to cheer him up.

"So, where is the menu? I'm hungry."

He raised his eyes to meet mine as their corners lifted. "There are no menus here. They have someone whose job is to saite the future and see the meal we would enjoy best, and that is what they will serve us. All restaurants here are like that. I can't believe you have been in the faction all this time and didn't know it was how we did things."

"I'm not a fan of fancy restaurants, and whenever I visited a place to grab a bite, they always suggested something that I quickly accepted. I thought it was their way to help me try the faction's food, but now that I'm thinking about it, I realize that I haven't seen a menu since I came here."

"Why would there be?"

"Does this mean we never get to choose?"

Matso shook his head.

I tilted my head for a second. "My faction should create a post like that in Lunar and open immigration to Delphians who would like to fill it." I looked into Matso's eyes. "Do you know how long it takes just to decide on your entree? Perhaps half of the evening."

He chuckled. "That sounds like fun, though."

"What? No." I shook my head. "It's annoying. We waste most of the evening deciding on something, then halfway through the meal, we think we should have ordered something else. Here we get to focus on one another, and we're sure it will be the best meal we could have ordered, as you said. Sorry if I sounded like I was complaining earlier. I was just wondering."

"I get it, but it must be fun to have choices sometimes."

"Oh." I saw how his eyes became a little vacant and wondered about his words, realizing how something so small could have such meaning to a different culture. It may be indeed annoying to spend the time choosing, but at least we know it was our choice.

I wondered what else in his life made him feel like he had no choice, and at that moment, I felt the need to vanquish his doubts. I knew it would also help my plan, but I didn't care much about that. I just genuinely wanted him to be happy.

"Why don't you try to ask the waiter about what they have, and you choose from that?"

"Okay, let me saite, and I will see his answer. It will be better than actually calling him."

"No." I put my palm on the table near Matso with a sudden move. "Don't saite anything. Call him here and ask."

"There's no need to waste his time."

"We're not wasting anyone's time. These people work in the restaurant. We are only asking them to do their job."

He smiled, slipping his hand to the top of the table and taking hold of mine. "Thank you."

I shifted my gaze to his hand, then back to his face. He appeared happy, and I thought there was no harm in letting him hold my hand for a while, but he didn't let go until the waiter came to our table.

When the server arrived, he handed Matso a piece of paper with the restaurant's dishes handwritten on it.

"That was quick." I raised my brows.

Matso chuckled. "You said I couldn't saite, but he could. He saw what I was going to ask about and prepared the answer." He looked into my eyes. "What do you want?"

"Me?" I smiled. "I'm used to choosing, so I want to see what they will bring me, but you can choose whatever you want from that piece of paper."

"I don't know what to choose. It all sounds good. I like chicken, but the beef comes with curry sauce. I never had beef with curry before." He scratched his forehead. "Or maybe river fruits. That sounds good too."

I watched him struggling to choose and couldn't help but smile. He looked so cute. He had a wide grin I was almost sure he didn't realize he carried.

About ten minutes later, he put the paper on the table. "Okay, I will go with beef." He paused. "Or maybe—"

He reached for the paper again, but I quickly put my hand on it. "No, we won't do this the whole night." I smiled, teasing him. "You have to make your choice right now."

He nodded and reached for my hand again, only this time he held it with both of his. "Final decision, beef." His grin widened.

"Call for the waiter then," I said with a smile.

"Oh no, he won't come again. They will see what I chose and make it, but at least this way, I know I made my choice." He gently pressed on my hand and met my gaze. "How do you feel in Delphia so far?"

"Nothing to complain about yet."

"Do you see yourself living here forever?"

"I don't know about forever, but for now, I have no choice."

We talked for a while until the waiter came with our entrees. That was when I realized that I forgot my hand was in Matso's all that time, so I gently pulled it back. The rest of the evening went well, exceptionally good actually, in that I didn't ask him anything about his special power. I didn't forget, but I was enjoying the conversation and didn't want to change it. Either way, I knew I had the time, and the deeper he felt our connection was, the more he would tell me.

That night he insisted on escorting me back to my house outside the city. I didn't want him to think that I would invite him in, but I decided to go with the flow.

When we reached the house, he waited down the three stairs leading up to the entrance even though I climbed them.

"I had a lovely evening tonight," he said before I turned to look at him. "I would like it if we could do it again sometime."

"Well..." I paused. "We don't have to always go to the same restaurant. You could show me other activities that your faction offers. After all, I have already used up half my time inside the city for this month as per your leadership rules."

"Of course." He nodded with a smile, ignoring my last statement. "Goodnight, Oran. I'll see you soon."

"Goodnight," I said and turned toward the door. But after I opened it, I turned back again and called for him. "Can I ask you something?"

"Anything." He took a step closer to me.

"Can you not saite to see what will happen between you and me? Leave it for the universe to surprise us." I widened my eyes in a playful way. "Please?"

"As I said earlier, with you, I never have." He smiled, then turned away and shouted, "Goodnight, beautiful Oran."

I genuinely smiled then, even though I knew that my question was mean and solely for my own benefit.

SAITE LAND

Over the following month, Matso and I met nearly every day. He wanted to teach me everything about the culture of Delphia, and I, of course, let him. He told me how the children learn saiting in school, how it's against the law for Delphians to explore the lower streets of their own city, and that he, like everyone else, never saw the skyscrapers from down below. However, what I loved most about Delphia was their popular board game, which we played nearly every night, yet I never won.

"Tonight is the night," I said, walking into our regular hangout spot, a small open space between two large trees where the grass was already dead. We always sat on the ground, our backs resting against the large, curved log of a fallen tree, with a fire burning not far from us.

Matso said nothing and pointed at the board opposite him. Rubbing my forehead, I playfully narrowed my eyes and took my place on the other side of the board, my legs crossed on the ground.

He set up the game then pointed at the board. "Your move," he said.

The game was simple. There were twenty tokens on a white board. Ten red and ten black. Matso had already set up the game by placing the tokens in two parallel lines that started at his side and ended on mine. On every line, the colors interchanged so no two tokens of the same color were next to one another. The goal was for each player to take all his tokens off the board without the other noticing. The problem with this game for me was that it was designed specifically for people who can see the future and are able to anticipate every move of their opponent. Therefore, Matso had the upper hand. But I had been listening carefully to every explanation he gave me about his power, and that night, I believed I finally had a plan.

"Let's do this," I said, rubbing my hands together.

Nodding, he flipped the hourglass with his eyes focused on the board.

"So much tension, and we didn't even start yet." I chuckled. "Take it easy, Matso."

"Right, so you can steal all your tokens in one move. I won't fall for that," he said without a flinch.

"Maybe you should go easy on me for a change," I moved my left hand toward the first token with a slow movement. "For example, you should let me take this—"

"Busted," he said, grabbing my other hand, which was formed into a fist after I had moved it as fast as I could toward the token at the top right. "Now you have to put it back, and since this was your first and you don't have an extra token to return, I get double time for my turn."

"That would, of course, be true if I had something in the hand you grabbed." I flipped my fist and opened it, revealing an empty palm.

"Huh... Well, it doesn't matter. You still took nothing off the board, and your time is over." He pointed at the small hourglass on the ground.

"Perhaps," I said with a wide grin, pushing my back against the log.

Matso's eyes widened when he saw I only had seven pieces left on the board. "That's impossible, I saited all your possible moves, and in every timeline, you reached for the tokens with your right hand."

"I thought we agreed that you won't saite anything relating to us."

"No, no." He shook his head. "This rule doesn't apply to the game. Saite Land is all about reading the future. Two players who try to defeat one another based on who can saite faster."

"And you know I don't have your power."

"Not my fault. I explained to you how the game works the first time we played it, and you insist on challenging me night after night."

"Well, obviously, you're not as great of a saiter as you claim since I just defeated you." He wasn't wrong, though. I had indeed picked up the tokens with the hand he caught, but my plan was working. I finally realized that the only way for him to not see my move in his future is if he doesn't see it at all and that I must never explain to him how I did it. To do that, I needed to use the power of my seeds. What Matso didn't know was that when I rubbed my forehead, I was, in fact, brushing my purple seed to activate it and make it react faster to my thoughts. While my fist cradled the three tokens, I manipulated my skin the same way I do to change the look of my clothes. Only this time, I hid the tokens under a piece of clothing that imitated the exact color and shape of my skin, making my palm appear empty when I unfolded it.

Matso's forehead curled as he became even more serious about the game after that, and even though I successfully used the same technique again, he managed to clear the board within two turns with five of my pieces still in the game.

As time moved forward, I found myself enjoying his company more and more, but I could never feel toward him the way he wanted me to feel, so I used the pull-push technique. Whenever things started to get serious, I pushed him away, and when he started to feel upset, I pulled back. The technique was working well, but I couldn't use it for much longer. He was starting to notice, and I didn't want him to realize I was manipulating him for information. However, there were times I didn't feel manipulative at all and would actually want him close to me. He did fill a big hole in my heart that Lunar left, and I would have struggled not to sneak out of Delphia if he wasn't there. His presence made me feel at home, and trying to get information out of him gave me a purpose. I was a spy again, doing what I do best.

By the end of my fifth month in Delphia, I had learned a lot about Matso. I understood everything about his side power as much as he did himself. I also knew the complete duties of his job and every little detail inside his duplex apartment. However, there was one thing he never wanted to talk about, his childhood.

No matter what angle I approached the subject with, he always shut it down. I began to believe his darkest secrets were there, and I was determined to know them all.

While getting ready to go and meet him one day, my purple seed blinked. My heart raced, and I accidentally poked myself with my earring because I knew what the blinking meant. I was receiving a call from Lunar. With my eyes on my reflection in the mirror, I wondered whether to accept or ignore the call, but my curiosity decided for me.

I brushed the seed and saw the caller appear in a full-size hologram image in front of me. All our seeds are connected to the heart of the white lotus, and that gave us an internal network to communicate with one another. In the old days, Lunardis used to communicate through the blue seed by transferring thoughts. When we realized that we could use the purple seed, which manipulates shapes and transforms surfaces into anything we think of, it became easier. Combining the power of both seeds gave us the ability to construct our thoughts, visuals, and imagination into one image that we could then transfer to the other person's seed, who could then see and talk to their contact as if the two were in the same place, regardless of the distance.

When I saw the hologram take the complete shape of the caller, I released a sigh, relieved to see who it was, even though my heart still raced a little.

"Bodya!" I raised my brows. "I didn't expect to see you again."

"I told you I would call when I checked on the control seeds I gave you."

"Right." I smiled. He was as handsome as ever, and my heart shook every time I saw him. "Did you fix them?"

"Maybe. Can you get them, please?"

"Okay, but it will have to be quick. I'm meeting someone." I moved to my bedroom, where I had stored the box he gave me, his hologram image floating to my side.

"A date?" He smiled, but I could feel he was forcing it. Nonetheless, the smile never left his face, and I decided to ignore the way it made me feel.

"I'm just meeting the correspondence official." I don't know why I didn't tell Bodya it was a date. He was talking as if it meant nothing to him, and I should have done the same.

"Right, diplomacy stuff." He smiled again, and this time, it felt genuine. "Make us proud."

I nodded. "I have the seeds now." I opened the box.

"Can you please attach the first one from the right to your blue seed?"

I did.

"Try to control something, any appliance."

I did, but nothing happened, "It's not working" I shook my head. "I'm in a hurry, Bodya."

"This will be just a minute, I promise."

He looked like he was turning something, but I didn't know what since I could only see him and not his surroundings.

"How are things in Delphia?" He spoke with his eyes on whatever he held in his hands. "Do they like having you there as a diplomat?"

"They love me here."

"I see." He stopped what he was doing. "Why don't you try the one next to the seed you just used?"

I did. "Still nothing, but I really have to go. Can we do this later?"

"Of course." He excused himself and disconnected the call.

I rushed out of the house. Usually, I walked back into the city. It was a thirty-minute walk to the elevator by the entrance, the one that took me up to the rooftops, but I started to feel sick after the call, so I pulled out my lotus pod to fly myself there.

While on my pod, I began to feel even worse. My head started spinning, and my eyelids grew heavier. Feeling the weight of my brain, I leaned my back against one of the lotus petals forming the shape of my pod. Once I rested my head, my eyes closed on their own, and I found myself somewhere else.

CAREFUL WHAT YOU WISH FOR

Even though my eyes were closed, I could feel the wind crash against my skin as my body remained in my pod. However, the fresh sensation of the air quickly became crushing, and my brain grew heavy before my mind replaced all my senses with a world of its own.

Lost inside my brain, my surroundings became clear as if I had teleported to another dimension where my imagination and memories collided.

An uncontrollable smile grew on my face the moment I opened the door to my apartment, only this time it looked different. The lifeless walls I was used to had vanished as decorations breathed a sense of home into the small place. Frames of family pictures with Bodya and I centered two canvases of abstract art on one wall, while a large glass cupboard filled most of the opposite one, its inside packed with plates, glasses, and utensils. An oval table with a glass top centered a red and blue carpet with an artistic style similar to that of the canvases. Around the table, two large sofas edged the carpet.

Inhaling deeply, I smelled rosemary and thyme infused with my favorite scent of a perfectly roasted chicken. Following the smell, I moved into the kitchen, where I heard instrumental music, the sound becoming louder as I moved closer. My brows drew together when I saw Bodya tending to the food on the stove, yet my body leaned against the door with a relaxed pose as if I knew he would be there.

I stood in silence, watching him work, my arms crossed against my chest, then moving to my sides before changing their position again. Like my body language, I wasn't sure if I was happy or surprised, but when he turned in my direction, my jaw dropped. Even though I was sure I was looking at Bodya's back, it wasn't him in the kitchen. Instead, I saw Matso, and the way he smiled could only mean that it was normal to see me there.

Surprised, I wanted to go back to the living room and inspect the family photos one more time, but my body refused to follow my instruction, and all I could do was stand still, my eyes focused on Matso with a strange feeling of love in my stomach.

"I thought you would be in my arms by now," Matso said while walking around the table that centered the kitchen.

I didn't know what to say, but I didn't have the chance to speak after my legs moved on their own and ran toward him. Jumping on Matso, my body continued to move on its own until my lips were on top of his. I wanted to pull away, but my body continued to defy me, reuniting our lips again and again. When a timer rang, my body shivered, and everything turned black.

**

Still hearing the timer, I sat up with a sudden move before opening my eyes. My pod was floating above the forest, the lights of Delphia's skyline clear in the distance.

My mind told me that I couldn't keep going through this every time I saw Bodya, that my heart needed to understand that this relationship had ended a long time ago.

At that moment, I became aware that the taste of Matso's kisses was still on my mouth, but when I touched my lips with the tip of my fingers, I realized they tasted exactly like Bodya's, bringing back thoughts of our old relationship and pulling me away from reality again. As I fell back into my thoughts, the timer sound gradually became stronger, and my mind pulled me back to the kitchen with my legs wrapped around Matso.

***

Knowing how much I craved for Bodya's lips and their sweet taste, my brain no longer fought back as Matso and I continued to kiss. The more our faces remained on top of one another, the more I wanted Matso. Once I surrendered myself to the moment entirely, my mind drove me through another scenario where I felt happy in my life.

And like the first scene, it always started with Bodya bringing out my best feelings before I found myself in Matso's arms again, and again, and again until the loop finally spit me out.

***

When I opened my eyes for the last time, my perspective returned. Yet, all I could think about was how I was late meeting Matso, and I pushed my pod to its top speed.

WHAT THE HEART WANTS

On my way to Matso, I thought of nothing but him and how I couldn't wait for his lips to meet mine, this time for real. When I stepped off my pod, several feet away from him, I smiled as our eyes met. He was waiting for me by the entrance of a rooftop park. Looking at him, I became mad at myself for dragging things further than they needed to go.

The moment my pod retreated into a seed, and I put it back in my body, I rushed to him, and smashed my lips to his for a kiss that I believed was overdue.

At first, the kiss felt strange and not exactly as I had anticipated, but the longer it lasted, the more I felt I was doing the right thing.

"That," he said, looking a little dizzy, "was better than I could have ever imagined."

"I'm sorry it took me so long to realize what I wanted."

"Don't be." He held my hand. "I would have waited for years if it meant I could have one taste of your lips."

I rubbed his arm with my free hand, and we walked into the park together. I was genuinely happy that night. The park was perfect too. From its edge, we could see the clouds below us and the bright stars above. We laid on the grass, our hands still connected and closed our eyes. We said nothing for hours, just stayed there until they kicked us out to close the park.

As usual, Matso walked me home, but this time was different. That night I invited him in. I wanted to offer him something to drink before I smoothly transitioned us into the bedroom, but I couldn't wait for him to be in my arms. I felt as if we had been in love for a long time and were lost from one another, but that night, we found each other again, defying all the odds that broke us apart.

The moment he sat on a chair, I jumped on him, placing his legs between my thighs. I slid my fingers into his smooth hair and placed the other palm on his cheek before I moved in for a kiss. Our tongues danced, getting a feel for one another until I realized that I didn't feel any of his hands on my body. Pulling my head back, I glared at his arms and the way he placed them outside the chair before I locked my gaze with his. Uttering nothing, I smiled and gave him a quick peck on the nose before I brushed my purple seed, making all my clothes disappear, and his eyes bulged out.

"Were you...?" he asked, unable to finish the question.

"Always naked?" I finished it for him. "It depends on how you see it. If you base it only on your concept of clothing, then yes. Lunardis are always naked."

"They just look so real."

I placed a finger on his lips. "In a way, they are, and they do the job, but we're not here to talk about how my clothing works." I tugged on the bottom of his white shirt. "We are here to lose them." I took it off.

I moved in for another kiss but felt a hint of a struggle. "What now?" I pulled my head back again, only this time I showed him my frown.

"It's just..." He lowered his chin. "This is my first time."

"Oh." I raised my brows. "Then this is not a good place for a first-timer." I stood and grabbed his hand, then pulled him to my bedroom upstairs.

***

The following morning, I woke up before him. I leaned on my side and rested my cheek on my hand as I looked at the beauty in my bed. I knew it was strange and didn't make sense, but I couldn't help but feel that we had been in love for a long time. I was happy, so I stopped thinking about it.

"Good morning, handsome," I said the moment he opened his eyes, placing my free hand on his chest. "Last night didn't feel like someone who was doing this for the first time."

He slipped a hand under my side and pulled me in for a long kiss that evolved into a long passionate morning, afternoon, and night. In fact, it lasted for a week, and it only ended because he ran out of excuses to escape his job.

***

When Matso left my place, and I found myself alone again, I started to think about what was going on and why my brain was playing these games on me when it had never done so before. My initial thought of it being a side effect of me losing my seeds resurfaced in my mind. However, I realized that these strange images dominated me only after I saw Bodya. First, after seeing him in the garden of my house, and the second time when he called me through our seed connection. I wondered if it would still happen, now that my feelings for Matso were clear and I had finally felt that I moved on with my life.

I tapped my purple seed twice and thought about Bodya. A few seconds later, he responded to the call, and I could see him.

The moment his body fully transpired opposite me, my heartbeat trembled again, just like it did every time my eyes fell on him.

"Is everything okay?" He took a step closer to me, and I could feel he wished he could touch me.

I sighed loudly and looked at him in silence for a moment. "I just wanted to check on something."

"Are you in danger?" He drew his brows together.

"I'm not. It's just...You are a scientist, right? What do you know about the side effects of losing our seeds?"

"What do you mean?"

"I was wondering if losing our six seeds for a day or two had side effects."

"Like what?" he asked, his eyes narrowed.

"I don't know, like seeing images that are not true."

"Not that I know off. According to our data, your body will start reacting to the absence of the seeds five weeks after their disappearance. And even then, it will take six months to a year before your body fails entirely and dies. However, if you got your seeds back in that time, you should be able to return to normal. So, no, I don't think losing your seeds for a few days has any side effect."

"Then, why..." I stopped, realizing that Bodya wasn't the only present factor whenever I had the strange images. I pulled the box of seeds he gave me from the nightstand and waved it at him. "What are these?" I asked, my voice rising to its edge.

"Like I told you—"

"Stop." I interrupted him. "Your body language tells me that whatever you will say next is going to be a lie. Tell me the truth right now. I won't ask another time."

"It's safer if you don't know," he said, lowering his voice.

"I will decide that on my own, thank you very much."

"Fine, but promise me you will be careful." He ran his fingers through his hair, his face turning red.

"I will promise you nothing!" I shouted. "You, however, owe me for manipulating me."

He released a sigh. "We took away parts of your memory, so the Delphians don't see what you're up to. We then put some of these memories into the glass seeds and planned each one carefully, so you have enough information to pursue your mission without putting yourself in danger."

My head jerked upward, and my body took a step back, my heartbeat rising. "What are you talking about?"

"You went to Delphia on a mission, and—"

"That can't be. I escaped after Nerva framed me, and the protectors took away my seeds."

"I know, but all of that was part of the plan."

"Whose plan?"

"Ours."

"Ours as in you and—"

"As in you and me," he answered before I finished.

"How can that be when you and I didn't spend any time together since our breakup?"

Bodya scratched his scalp, and his gaze lowered. "I guess since you know that much, there's no point in delaying the inevitable, not anymore." He met my eyes. "Why don't you take the seed next to the one you last used and put it on your blue seed."

I chuckled. "So, you can manipulate me even further. No, thank you."

"I'm not trying to manipulate you, I promise. Those seeds carry the memories we suppressed, and using them puts those lost memories back into your brain."

"You mean what I see actually happened?" My brows raised.

He nodded. "Just give it a try."

I looked at the box in my hand and took a deep breath. My heart continued to race as I focused on the small glass seeds before picking up the one he asked me to use.

I turned my gaze back to him. "Bodya, I swear by the name of the lotus, if—"

"I'm the one who's swearing to you right now that everything I said is true."

Sighing, I put the glass seed on my blue one.

"Perhaps it's better if you sit. The journey might be rough."

Listening to his advice, I walked to my bed and sat on it while the usual migraine that hit me every time I used those seeds began to take control over my brain. My eyelids started to react the same way too, but this time I closed them first, anticipating what was about to happen.

THE TRUTH WE FEAR

After a few minutes of lying on my bed with my eyes closed, a palette of paint colors began falling out of nowhere, slowly spreading into the blackness and altering my understanding of reality. Moments later, I found myself inside the director's office, my brain believing it was the day I met Matso for the first time in my faction, along with his two Delphian colleagues who came to the headquarters. I examined my surroundings for a moment then turned to my boss, who threw a file in front of me. It was the same image I saw after Bodya handed me the first seed when we met by my house. Only this time, the conversation continued until the director gave me the mission to investigate Matso before my brain thrust me into another scene where Bodya explained the memory seeds before getting pulled back to the director's office.

With my memories back, the picture became clear, and Bodya's words didn't sound as crazy as before, and the more I saw, the more I knew them to be true. Yet, something was wrong. Amidst the memories I saw, there were others that didn't make sense. Matso and I walking through the streets of Lunar hand in hand, or us spending multiple nights in my apartment.

When the blackness returned to my eyes, I opened them and sat up, my gaze instantly falling on Bodya's hologram. He was standing still, looking back at me, but it was clear he wanted me to talk first. However, I didn't. Instead, I stepped off the bed and paced the room a few times, thinking about what I saw before finally returning to Bodya again.

I started. "So, all of this was—"

"Part of the plan."

"Infiltrating Kala?"

"The director gave them a fake story about how you escaped and that we suspected you were going there. He told them that if they gave you back to us, our faction would completely ignore them killing two of our people a few weeks prior. When Mydon brought you back, the director and I were hiding, and once he subdued you with the sedative we gave him, we picked up your body."

"What if Kala had killed me instead of sending me back?"

"You agreed to take the gamble, but the director was never worried."

"And my seeds? I never really lost them, did I?"

"Yes, you did, but only for a moment. Everything you saw since leaving for Kala was real. However, the part that happened in Lunar was theatrical. You supervised every detail yourself, and it was you who insisted that we take away your seeds. You said it was the only way to make you believe that Lunar was too dangerous for you, that if we followed any other tactic, your instinct would be to stay and fight back until you proved your innocence."

"That does sound like me." I took a deep inhale and breathed it out in a single exhale. "Poor Nerva. All this time, I thought she was the traitor."

"It was part of the job. She knew that you would get your memories back eventually and understand the truth. Don't worry about her."

"Still." I crossed my arms over my chest and glanced at the ground. "In one of the memories, you said the glass seeds might have a side effect. Did you figure that out?"

Bodya shook his head. "We didn't use it on anyone else. It's you who should tell me."

I pursed my lips in a fine line. "Could they, for example, make me realize my true feelings to someone?" I asked, then quickly added. "Or something?"

"I'm not sure I follow."

"Can the seeds affect my emotions somehow?"

"I don't know." He paused, stroking his chin for a minute before nodding. "It's possible, yes."

"How?" I quickly asked, my eyes glued to him.

"Well, it depends. Can you tell me why it is you're asking this question?"

"No, I'd rather just hear your theory about it."

He nodded, but I could tell he wasn't happy about my answer, yet he continued with the explanation. "While the heart is known to be the center of emotions, in truth, feelings are based on brain stimulation. And your brain defines the feeling based on experience. In other words, the cumulation of your memories decides what you think makes you happy or sad. However, those emotions are carved in your brain at a young age, and the truth is, it's a lot more complicated than that, but that's the only connection I see between memories and feelings."

"No, that's not what I was talking about."

"If you just tell me—"

"I said no, Bodya. I won't tell you."

He lowered his head.

"I have another question, though."

"Whatever you need."

"How is it that we are talking again. Other than the memories of you helping me with the mission, I don't remember us ever being in contact since our breakup."

Bodya narrowed his eyes. "That shouldn't be the case. Every seed I gave you since we met at your house contains an individual memory of us."

"Individual? Did we get back together or something?" I said with a sarcastic tone, but Bodya didn't pay attention to me. Instead, he began fidgeting with something in front of him, repeating what went wrong to himself multiple times.

"Hey." I clapped. "Bodya. Focus here," I said, and he finally returned his gaze to me. "Why don't you just tell me what happened?

He looked at me in silence then shook his head. "I think it's better that you don't know anyway. At least for now. This information doesn't affect your mission in any way. When you get the rest of your memories back, I will tell you everything."

I heard the sentence "the rest of my memories" repeat itself in my brain, and I ran to the seed container, picked it up, then grabbed the last seed. "Are the last of my missing memories in here?"

He nodded.

"Fine, then I will just use it and get the answers I need myself."

"Don't!" he shouted, trying to reach for my hand, seemingly forgetting that we were both only holograms to one another.

"Why?" I asked, my brows forming a V. "I already know about the mission. The plan is complete."

"Yes, you know everything about the mission, but you are still a spy. The last seed contains sensitive information about the faction that you agreed to keep away until you are about to leave Delphia."

"You don't understand, Bodya. Right now, I feel that something is missing, and I need to know if the answer is in the seed."

"I'm sorry that you feel like this, but the information on this seed could potentially put other people in danger, such as your own..." He paused. "Trust me, you want to keep them safe."

I sighed.

"Where are you on your mission anyway? Did you find the information we need about Matso?"

"Not yet." My head jerked back a little. I didn't know why I lied. It wasn't my intention. "I need more time. He may be hiding something."

"You can do it, Oran. I believe in you." My eyes narrowed at his words, but he didn't seem to notice as he continued. "Just don't use the last seed until you are leaving Delphia, please."

"Fine, I will wait, but I'm not sure for how long, and maybe it will be better if you don't reach out until I contact you myself."

"As you wish. All I ask is that you be careful."

Nodding, I cut our connection and crawled back into my bed. Learning that my faction didn't see me as a traitor and that I could go home whenever I wanted brought back a sense of peace I had forgotten I could even feel.

I took a moment to digest all the information I just discovered and process the truth about my life, but as I sat in silence, all I could think about was Matso. I wondered if this mission was fair for him and if it was his fault that he saw his future with me. Then again, all my faction wanted was some information, and they entrusted me with this job.

With my back on the bed, I held the remaining seed between my fingers and raised it to the length of my arms. My gaze focused on the small piece of glass at the tip of my fingers, and for the first time, I noticed a hint of blue at its center. I brought the seed near one eye and closed the other to focus on the details. At first, I saw nothing, but the more I looked at it, the more I felt as if I was looking at the center of the universe. Such a small piece was both beautiful and deadly.

I wondered whether the seed would give me the answers I needed or just add more questions. However, I didn't dwell on the question for long. I knew how dangerous it was to focus on the unknown when the only path is to make a decision and stick to it. That was my dilemma, though, the decision.

My options were clear. I could either stick with the mission, find the last piece of information about Matso's childhood, and return home where I would cement my name as the greatest spy, or follow my heart and see where my life with Matso would take me.

In the past, when I found myself blocked by feelings, I would remove my red seed to dampen my emotions and move on with my mission but seeing Bodya multiple times reminded me of how happy I was when we were in love and how dull my out-of-work life became since we parted ways. And now, I was facing the same choice Bodya forced me into five years prior.

"Love or spy?" I muttered, tossing the seed up in the air. "Spy or love?" I tossed it again.

As I captured the seed midair, I knew how to decide. Stepping off the bed, I rushed down to the living room and grabbed a token off the board of Saite Land, which was still on the dining table since my last game with Matso. The token had the letter S carved on one side and a plain surface on the other.

"Okay, Oran," I said to myself. "S is for spy, and empty is for love." I took a deep breath and tossed the token high in the air, my eyes following its movement and rotation. As the token fell, I snatched it out of midair. I finally had my answer.

PART FOUR

Path of Life

ONE FOOT DOWN

Once I made my decision, I contacted Matso. It was time to put everything on the table and play the last card. I asked him to meet me at the first restaurant he took me to, the one with green walls and golden decorations.

When I saw him by the entrance, I kept a small smile on my face. As usual, his white suit and brown collar suited him, especially after adding a lotus flower button at the top of his suit that matched the color of his blue leather shoes. It was a small detail, but I liked it. The moment I became within his reach, he lifted my hand and planted a kiss on it.

"You look as beautiful as ever, Oran." His gaze slid down to my blue dress, which fell just short of my knees before he returned to my eyes.

"You're not bad yourself."

"Shall we go in?" He shaped his arm in a half circle for me to slide mine inside. When we went in, I realized that he had asked for the same table we had the first time, another detail that I enjoyed.

"So, this is a serious meeting, isn't it?" he asked while pulling out a chair for me.

I nodded and sat.

He took the opposite seat. "Are you leaving Delphia?"

"What makes you ask that?" My eyes widened.

"What could be more serious than your departure?"

I lifted one corner of my mouth for a second. "First, I want you to know the truth about me, then we can talk about what will happen next."

"I'm listening."

"You know that I'm a spy."

"And the best as you always say." He chuckled. "But that's in the past now, right?" He focused on my eyes, and I looked away.

"Well, the truth is," I said, keeping my gaze away from his, "I'm still a spy. My faction never shunned me. It was all a play to break into yours." I glanced at him through the corners of my eyes to see his reaction, but there was none. His face was empty, and I realized he wanted to wait until I spelled all I had to say.

I told him everything about the mission. When I received it, how we planned it, and how the memory seeds helped shield me from their power of saiting.

"Why are you telling me this now?" he asked. "Is your—" He paused when the waitress entered our private space to put our food on the table, then continued when she left. "Do you want to rub it in my face that your mission is complete? Or do you enjoy seeing other people's hearts break?"

A tear escaped to slide down my cheek. "I don't want to break your heart."

"Then why did you tell me?" he shouted, banging his hands on the table. The other guests looked at us when they saw his reaction, but it was clear they couldn't hear him because of the sound barrier surrounding us.

"Because I love you." I blinked back the second tear and heaved a heavy sigh. "I gave up on love for my career before, and while I don't regret that decision, I have always wondered how my life would be if I took the other route. This time, I want to see where this would take us." I pointed at the two of us. "I want to become the traitor I never wanted to be and go rogue for you."

I tried to reach for the hand he had on the table, but he pulled away. Sighing, I continued. "This decision is not easy for me, and you, of all people, must know that. You know the faction laws and, more importantly, how I feel about not being able to go home. Yet, I'm giving it all up for a feeling."

"And how do I know this is not another manipulative technique of yours. It could easily be the last step in your plan."

"Saite me."

"What?" He drew his brows together.

"Saite me and see if the rest of my life is here or not. If I will leave in the future, you can see it." I paused. "It's best for both of us. Perhaps, you can tell me where my life will take me so we can end this agony once and for all."

Uttering nothing, he leaned back in his chair and closed his eyes for a few minutes. I didn't know if he was calming himself or looking into the future, but I waited until he wanted to speak. When he grinned, I knew he believed me.

He opened his eyes, his expression relaxed again. "Are you sure you're okay with your decision?"

"I am."

He nodded. "I'm sorry I snapped at you, and I can see that you are speaking the truth. However, there's something that you need to know. If you keep the final seed in your position, we will never have a happy life. I inspected several timelines, and you never use it. Yet, it stays in your mind, feeding it doubts. You will never stop wondering about the memories you didn't get, and that will make you...us...miserable. I don't want a life with you if it will bring you pain. On the other side, if you were to get rid of it—"

"Was I happy?" I interrupted. "When I let go of it, did you see us happy?"

"I can see up to a decade, Oran, and I can for sure tell you that yes, we will be happy, very happy, but only if you make the right decision."

I closed my eyes for a moment before reaching into my pocket, pulling the glass seed out, and placing it on the table between us. "Take it."

"Are you sure?"

Gazing at the seed, I shook my head. "I'm not, but you're right. My brain won't go silent until I see the end of this path. Take it. Destroy it. I will worry about the future later."

With a slow movement, he lifted the seed and put it in his pocket. "Since you trusted me with your secret and are willing to stay here for me, then you deserve to know my secret too."

"You don't have to tell me anything."

"I want to." He looked into my eyes. "This will be the first time I share the secret with someone willingly, but I'm ready." He took a deep breath. "I'm a half breed."

My eyes grew wide, but it made sense. This was why he knew so much about mixed children during the orientation and seemed to be affected by it. I said nothing, though. I was more interested in what he had to say next.

"My father was a Delphian, but my mother was from Averett. They met after a group of Averettis tried to infiltrate my faction. My father was one of the guards who trapped and executed them. During the executions, my mother escaped, and it was my father who hunted her down. I'm not sure what happened after, but the story they told me a thousand times entails a supposed honorable act of my father."

Matso took a deep breath, his eyes pointing downward. "When my father finally caught up to her, he hurt her badly and killed one of her Majestics. Yet, mother ignored her wounds and lowered to her companion animal, taking it in her arms, asking only for her final death to be next to her beast. Her behavior, however, altered my father's perception, and he refused to take a soul that had compassion. Instead, he hid her inside a cave in the northern mountains and brought back her beast as proof of her death.

"Apparently, it didn't take long for them to fall in love after that, but they both knew what would happen if Delphia found out that my father lied or Averett knew that their tribe member abandoned her mission. The cave became their new home, and my father slowly faded his life out of the capital until he could move in with her. They had me two years later."

Matso released a broken sigh. "My entire childhood was in that cave. They banned me from going farther than a hundred feet outside." His body shivered, clearly remembering his past. "They should have known... They should have known that none of that mattered. They lived next to the lions' den, and the lions can see the future.

"Eventually, Delphia found out about them. The Skeptics executed my parents immediately but kept me alive. I was fifteen at the time, and they wanted to know how I survived. I moved from the cave to a prison where they ran all sorts of tests on me. For five years." He sighed again. "I was in that prison for five years until they decided my other power could help them. As they learned about my ability, so did I. It took time to master, but I could eventually read their thoughts."

His face reflected a smile of triumph. "I manipulated them, one by one, until I became the head of the correspondence office, but I won't stop there. One day, I will be the leader of this entire place, and I will punish those who forced my family to suffer." Matso closed his eyes and took a deep breath that he slowly exhaled with a faint shiver.

I didn't cry. I was good at keeping my emotions under control, but still, his story pained me. I couldn't imagine how I would have felt if I were in his place. I would have probably unleashed my inner beast on everyone.

He brought his gaze back to me. "Do you still want to be with me?" he asked, power building in his words.

"What?" My eyes widened. "Of course, I do. If anything, I want to be with you more."

"I love you, Oran. I knew I would love you from the first time I saw you."

"I... I feel the same way." It was the first time we exchanged the words, yet even though I felt them, I couldn't say them out loud. "Is that why your file had nothing when it came to Lunar?"

He nodded. "The file was empty because there's nothing to tell about me. They couldn't mention my life in the cave. To Delphia, I didn't exist before my last day in prison."

"I see. Well, let's eat because the food is getting cold, and I have a bed at home that won't be warm unless you are in it."

He smiled and took hold of my hand before planting a kiss on the tips of my fingers.

THE SINS WE CHOOSE

For the following seven months, I was happier than I could ever remember. Matso was great with me, and our love grew stronger every day. So strong that we didn't wait long for him to move in with me. He also pulled some strings to waive the limited time inside the city rule and replaced my civil service with a job at an entertainment firm that designs fun games for children.

At first, I thought the job would be boring but creating interactive games for little kids who could see the future proved challenging for me, and I grew to enjoy the daily obstacles. Things were going better than I hoped, and I was becoming more confident in my decision to stay every day, but then I received a call through my purple seed. One I knew would come sooner or later.

"Hello, Bodya, how are you?" I asked with a wide smile, my kitchen to my back and the dining table two feet from me, though he couldn't see any of that.

"I'm good. You look good too." He smiled back. "I take it your mission is going well?"

"Better." I looked into his eyes. "I called it off."

"I'm sorry, what?"

"You heard me correctly. I will no longer finish my mission."

"I don't understand. Does this mean you will come back?"

At that moment, Matso walked into the room, cementing my smile on my face. Bodya, of course, couldn't see him, so I wasn't surprised at his confused expression. Yet, I ignored him and tugged Matso's arm to bring him closer to me.

"What's going on?" Matso asked, his gaze focusing on Bodya's hologram. "Who is that?"

"That's Bodya, an old...colleague of mine."

"Who are you talking to?" Bodya asked.

"He can't see me?" Matso wondered.

"No," I responded to Matso. "Right now, he can only see a hologram of me wherever he is."

"He is not here?" Matso waved his hand through Bodya's body, nodding after touching only air. "Interesting. So, you can talk with your people without even being there."

"Wait, I will bring you in." I pulled a small seed out of my pocket and gave it to him. "Put it on your forehead."

When Matso did as I asked and his hologram appeared to Bodya, the latter took a step back. "What is he doing there?" Bodya asked.

"I live here," Matso answered.

Bodya's brows raised, and his face turned red. He seemed to stumble for words, but when Matso kissed my cheeks immediately after, Bodya fell into a seated position, perhaps in a chair on his end that I couldn't see.

"That can't be," Bodya said though it was clear he was only talking to himself, his eyes darting to the ground.

"As you can see, things have changed," I said, though Bodya's thoughts had clearly gone somewhere else.

"Impossible," Bodya said to himself again, but this time he scanned Matso and me, his face becoming more disturbed than I thought it would be. Rather than looking angry at my betrayal, he seemed to be more...broken. "You can't be with him. You are my—"

"She is happy," Matso interrupted Bodya, which I found strange considering how he never spoke for me.

"Happy?" Bodya whispered, his eyes becoming more and more vacant, his red seed blinking fast. "She is happy with—"

"I told you she is happy." Matso interrupted again, his voice louder. "Ask her yourself."

"It's okay, Matso." I pulled him to the back. "I can talk for myself."

"Then tell him. Tell him that this is the life you chose for yourself and that you are happy here."

I realized at that moment that Matso might be threatened by Bodya's appearance and afraid that I would change my mind about staying, so I took a step closer to him and cradled his cheeks. "Don't worry, love. No one can influence me. I made my decision already."

"What decision?" Bodya asked with a shout.

I turned to him, furious at his tone. "I told you already. I won't finish my mission. You know what, scratch that. Tell the director that the reason Matso's file was empty is because they knew nothing about him."

"Oran," Matso said.

"It's okay," I said to Matso, still looking at Bodya. "He lived outside the city where no one knew a thing about him his entire childhood. When he finally returned to the capital, he only went through an integration period. There's nothing else that you need to know and certainly nothing that threatens Lunar. "There. My mission is complete. Now, all you need to add in your report is that I won't be coming back."

Bodya shook his head as if struck by my words again. "You have to come back. At least for your—"

"Enough." I was the one who interrupted him this time. "I don't care what is waiting for me in Lunar. I will stay with Matso."

"This is not who you are. Trust me, Oran."

"That's Orantine to you, Bodya. And please know that I'm continuing with this call as a courtesy, but if you insist on disrespecting my wishes, then I will disconnect you."

Bodya bit his lower lip, and his blue seed started blinking. "The seed..." he said. "Did you use the last seed?"

"I did not."

"You must. Your last memories are there, and you will understand why you must return."

"Perhaps, but that doesn't matter anymore. The seed is no longer available."

"What?" Bodya's eyes bulged.

"She is right," Matso added. "I destroyed it already."

Bodya looked at me with veins popping on his forehead. "How could you throw your own memories away like that? This is not who you are."

"It is now, Bodya. This is what you need to understand."

"No." He shook his head violently. "You are the one who must remember who you are. You can't destroy us like that."

"Us?" My tone reached a higher octave. "There's no us, Bodya. It's my life, and only *I* get to decide what to do with it."

"No, it's not. You lost that luxury the day you had our—"

"Cut him off!" Matso shouted, his voice so loud that I didn't hear what Bodya said.

"Calm down." I turned to Matso with a stare. "I can talk for myself."

Bodya continued to speak, but Matso persisted with his shouting, and I failed to understand either of them.

"Enough!" I screamed, clenching my fists, and the two stood silent. "You," I said to Matso. "Go upstairs or something and let me handle this."

"But—"

"I said go." As Matso walked away, I turned to Bodya. "And you, I don't want to hear anything from you again. You wanted to know about the mission, and you got my answer. There's nothing more for us to talk about. Not now, not ever," I said and brushed my purple seed, dropping our connection.

Once Bodya's hologram disappeared, I reached into my mind through the blue seed and found the connection I had with the people in my faction. Using my thoughts, I severed the nerve that allowed other Lunardis to reach me to guarantee that none from my home faction could contact me again, not unless I decided to reverse the effect. It was my final act as I accepted that Delphia would now be my permanent home.

ONE LAST SECRET

Time passes quickly when you are happy. Days turn to weeks, then months and years. Seventeen years in Delphia passed like a single lightning strike. I had everything I wanted and believed it would last forever until I woke up the day before today.

Matso used to go to work much earlier than I did, so it wasn't strange when I opened my eyes, and he wasn't there. With music playing all over the house, I followed my morning routine as usual. I danced as I moved, and why wouldn't I? I was living the dream.

When I reached the kitchen to prepare my breakfast, I found an envelope on the countertop. I approached the letter with a smile, thinking it was another love letter like the ones Matso would leave me from time to time, but I didn't read it right away. Like always, I preferred to savor such moments, so I prepared my morning tea before taking both to my favorite spot on the couch.

With my mug in my hand and the music volume at a relaxing level, I pulled the letter out. Something else fell on the ground, startling me and nearly caused me to spill my tea. Quickly, I placed the cup on the small round table across from me and reached for the fallen item.

My heart raced as I saw what lay on the ground. It had been years since I saw the glass seeds of memory, and I had been under the impression none were left.

With my happy thoughts gone, I picked up the seed and looked at it for a moment, then placed it on the table, moving my gaze back to the letter. I wondered if it was Bodya who sent it to me, but the idea sounded impossible. I didn't dwell on my thoughts, knowing that all the answers I needed were in the letter I held in my hand, and I would have them if I read it, so I did, immediately recognizing Matso's handwriting.

My beautiful Oran,

I'm happy to have had you in my life. You brought me blessings far beyond what I could imagine, but life has a way of reminding us where everything truly belongs. Before you continue to the coming words, I want you to know that I loved you. I love you, and I will always love you, and this is why I'm revealing this to you now, the last secret.

The truth is, I knew about your mission all along. I orchestrated every move, calculated every word, and acted brilliantly to make you think that every thought you had and every action you did was yours. Even during Bodya's last call, I interfered in the right moments, saying the words that made sure you didn't listen to him, and he didn't push too hard on you, thus revealing the one thing that would have changed your mind.

I darted my eyes away from the letter, feeling every tremble in my heart as it raced against itself. I didn't know what would come next, but Matso had already said enough to force my red seed into blinking, and I had to continue reading, clinging to the hope that he was playing a game. A stupid game, it would be, but my dignity would still be intact, and my life wouldn't have been a lie. Wishing for that glimpse of light, I continued reading.

Nineteen years ago, the Skeptics saw a threat. A spy that managed to steal dark secrets that incriminated all the leaders of the faction in multiple horrendous crimes. That spy was you. You would have given the secrets to the Illicitums, so we had to act. The only way out was to neutralize you and keep you away from your faction for as long as possible.

You see, my love, I was never the head of correspondence. Like you, I'm a spy. You were my mission, and until today, I did it perfectly. I know you are wondering how I did it. I will tell you because I don't want you to suffer. That's how much I love you.

I studied you for a full year before making my first move, learning what makes you tick and what forces a reaction out of you. I remember I was jealous when I saw you and your husband in my saites.

"Husband?" I said the word out loud, reading it over and over. Confusion was the last thing I needed, but I had to know more. Ignoring my troubled breathing, I went back to the letter.

However, I quickly realized that your relationship was the answer. The way to breaking you was your heart. We created the asylum program especially for you, then sent altered research about genetic memory to your faction so Bodya could invent the memory seeds but fail to realize the side effects. I worked hard to make sure he didn't find out that the brain would react to incomplete memories by redirecting the faces to those closest to the subject. After that, my mission was easy. I faked the correspondence job and sent an empty report to your director, so he would give you the mission. I came to the meeting in your faction to direct your thoughts to the Kalangous council, so it would give you the idea to plant your memory seeds. I manipulated your every move. I was saiting you all the time to do the right thing and say the right words, even during our conversations.

My tears slid down my cheeks, but I continued to read.

You may be thinking now about the story of my parents. It wasn't a complete lie. I just changed the ending. You see, when the Delphian guards found us, they gave me a choice, to kill my parents and join their ranks or die with them. I wanted to get out of that cave and experience the world. It was my right to live.

I didn't lie about not being able to read your thoughts, though. I could at the beginning, but then I fell for you, and they became harder to decipher. That is the truth, and I should have told you a long time ago.

I'm telling you this now for two reasons. First, as I told you, half breeds always have complications, and mine came in the form of an illness that will stop my heart at any time within the next three years. Second, I received a letter from your husband yesterday, the one you gave up for me.

"He said husband again," I muttered to myself. Putting the letter down, I remembered Bodya's last call and how broken he seemed to be. I wondered if it was him who Matso spoke of. My gaze fell on the glass seed, and I grunted then kicked the table with my leg, shattering its glass top and bringing its contents to the ground, soaking the rug with hot tea. Clenching a fist, I lifted the letter again. I wanted to shred it to pieces, but I had to know. There was no other way.

He tried to contact you many times over the years, but I always made sure that none of his attempts were successful. However, this time he asked for my help, and after reading his words, I decided to give you the chance to choose what you want for yourself.

Your daughter is in trouble.

Tears streamed down my face as my eyes refused to believe the word "Daughter," but no matter how many times I read it, it remained the same.

Yes, you have a daughter, and she is as beautiful as you are. It seems she defied a video game company known as Lantrix and is trying to expose them for something. I'm not sure what it is exactly, but according to Bodya, they have a plan to eliminate her within three nights. He is not sure he can protect her for much longer but believes that you can save her.

That was my confession, one that I should have given you a while ago. As you can see, I never destroyed the last seed, as I told you I did. Use it. It will give you the rest of your memories, and everything will make sense. I won't be coming back today or any other day, but I know that if you want to find me, you will find a way.

May the future be always on your side, my love,
Matso

Curling the letter in my hand, I screamed, more tears covering my cheeks. "If I want to find him?" I cried. "If I ever find him, I will kill him with my bare hands."

I took a deep breath and caged my tears. He deserved none, and I needed to learn the whole truth. If I had a daughter, as he said and she was in danger, I needed to act quickly. I had no time for remorse.

GLASS MEMORY

I dropped the letter, retrieved the glass seed, put it on my blue one, and leaned against the back of the sofa. Within a short minute, the headache started, and even though I had already closed my eyes, I could still feel my lids growing heavy. The darkness started to fade away, and the new memories began to form as my brain took me to them.

THE LAST SEED

As I surrendered to my brain, it didn't take long for me to fall into the first memory. Once again, liquid paint descended out of nowhere, taking over the blackness surrounding my closed lids and constructing my new reality. Within moments I was no longer on my couch. Instead, I found myself on the beach of Lunar's capital. Someone was chasing me, but I didn't feel threatened. After a short run, I halted then turned while laughing. My chaser was Matso. I wanted to frown, but my face continued to smile. However, as he walked closer to me, his face started glitching, its features fading, then changing, then disappearing again before another face resurfacing and this time, it remained. The face was that of Bodya, an old Bodya that I knew too well. I felt sad in my heart, but my smile persisted, welcoming his arrival.

"You shouldn't run this fast, not for the next few months at least," Bodya said and put his palm on my stomach. "Not with life growing inside of you."

I put my hand on the back of his. "Don't worry about her. She is strong enough to handle a short run."

"How do you know the baby is a her?"

"A mother knows," I said, lifting his hand off my stomach, raising it to my lips, and kissing it. "You will see."

I wanted to scream inside, but my mind remained in control, peeling away the paint, replacing the memory with another. My body fell back, and I found myself lying on a hospital bed, screaming with my knees raised. A doctor was standing at my feet, his head nearly between my thighs.

"Push," the doctor said. "We just need one more."

Screaming to the edge of my lungs, I did as he instructed. The pain was too much, and I could feel it all over my body until I heard a baby cry. With the sound, all my agony vanished, and I started to breathe again. While trying to regulate my breathing, I lifted myself up to look at her, but the doctor had already placed her in an incubator.

"Is she okay?" I asked, my heart racing again, but this time not because of fatigue.

"She is. Don't worry. She just needs the lotus energy for her seeds to activate. It's a standard process that we have to do with every newborn."

I looked over at the incubator and the tubes coming out of it and reaching into the hospital walls. Bursts of white light flowed from the walls and toward my baby.

"Isn't she born with her seeds?" I asked.

"She is, but they won't work properly if she doesn't receive the life energy of the White Lotus."

I released a sigh of relief, finally understanding why it was against the law to give birth out of Lunar's general hospital. A few minutes later, the doctor brought my daughter to me. A smile grew on my face as I held her in my arms, but it quickly vanished when my eyes fell on her tiny seeds.

"Why are the colors of her seeds dull? Shouldn't they be glowing?"

"Relax, Miss Orantine. The seeds won't glow until she is six months old. It's perfectly normal. Now, why don't you tell me what you will call her?"

"Evailen," I said, my gaze focused on her perfect face, her cries bringing joy to my ears.

My brain once again pulled me into another memory. This time I was sitting on the edge of a black carpet inside my apartment. Bodya was at the other edge, and in his arms was one-year-old Evailen that he helped stand straight.

"Come, Evailen. Come to Momma," I said with a clap, my grin wide.

Bodya continued to support her with one hand, putting the other on her blue seed to help it send the signals to her brain. Evailen took a few steps and nearly fell, but Bodya secured his grip around her waist, stabilizing her. She took three more steps and nearly fell again, but this time, she seemed to balance herself though it was obvious that she still needed Bodya's help, who crawled behind her with every step she took.

When Evailen was one step away from me, she laughed, captivating my heart, and raised her two arms toward me. She nearly fell again, but I quickly snatched her up and held her, showering her with kisses.

When I landed in the next memory, I was carrying Evailen in my arm, a large frown on my face. She was eighteen months old.

"No," I said with conviction, taking a step backward, moving away from Bodya and toward the center of our living room.

"Come on, Oran. You will see her again, but you need to go."

"I said, no. I will tell the director that I can't do this mission."

"You refused a lot of missions for her. You told me yourself that your boss said if you don't do this one, he will have to put you on leave until you are ready to fully resume your job."

"Maybe it's for the best. I will ask him for a desk job or one of those less than-a-week missions he's been giving me over the last year. I can't go away for a full month."

"Nothing will happen, and I will be here to take care of her."

"I know, but what if I miss seeing her learning a new skill for the first time." I shook my head. "I can't do it."

Bodya relaxed his shoulder, the corners of his eyes lifting. "You can't always be there for her. You said that yourself when you got pregnant, and we agreed that we wouldn't let a baby affect our future. Go to your job, Oran, and when you return, you can spend all the time you want with her."

Exhaling, I pulled her closer to my chest and kissed her soft cheek before whispering into her ears. "I have to go away for a little while, but don't you ever forget how much Momma loves you. And when I come back, I will bring you gifts from the Fantastic Forest.

This memory didn't peel away like the other ones, but paint still changed on the walls, adding portraits to it and changing its face. I was still in the room though I was now seated on the couch, my hands turning empty and Evailen appearing at the other side of the room. She was slightly older, taller, and talking.

"Momma," Evailen ran to me. She punched my legs several times amid my laughter until I lifted her and sat her on my thighs.

"What do you want?" I asked.

"You said I can aks for kift for netsweek."

I laughed again at her mispronunciations. "Only if you tell me how old you are becoming."

She raised three fingers and pushed them close to my eyes.

"Good girl," I said, planting a kiss on her lips. "Now, what do you want?"

"I want Patra."

"What is that?"

"Not what, Momma. Ou." She frowned, crossing her arms against her chest."

"Okay, okay. Who is that?"

"Patra is tha karatter in tha new game Papa gave me."

"Oh, is she the lead character?"

With her brows raised, Evailen nodded multiple times.

"And is that a doll of her that you want."

She shook her head. "No, in tha room, on tha wall."

"You want a painting of her on your bedroom wall?"

She nodded again.

"Don't you have enough game characters on your wall?"

"No," she said, raising her voice, her frown conquering her face a second time.

"Okay, okay. Let me talk with Papa, and we will see what we can do about it."

Her grin returned, and mine widened in reaction before my surroundings faded away.

In the following memory, I was kneeling by Evailen's bed, my gaze focused on her tiny features and a burning pain in my heart as tears slid down my face. I wanted to pull her off the bed and hold her in my arm, but I couldn't. She looked peaceful with a face bright like a white lotus. My red seed blinked, its rhythm irregular, but I remained still until Bodya's hand cupped my shoulder. When I turned to him, he leaned his head toward the door, and I nodded. My gaze fell back on my daughter, and I kissed her forehead gently before rising to my feet and walking backward, my progression slow, and my eyes focused on Evailen until my back bumped against the doorframe. I quickly balanced myself, paying attention to the noise while glancing at her to make sure she was still asleep. Tears slid down my cheeks as Bodya took hold of my hand and pulled me out of the room.

"I don't want to forget about her," I said with a sob, hiding my head in his chest.

"It's the only way we can guarantee the success of your mission, but more importantly, her safety. If the Delphians discovered that you crossed them and that you have a daughter, they could use her against you."

"I will never let that happen."

"Neither will I, but better safe than sorry."

I nodded, the top of my head scratching Bodya's chest.

He continued. "It will just be for a few months, and when you return, you can bring her a gift from Delphia like you always do on your missions."

"Will you tell her about me?"

"Every night." He kissed my forehead.

I wiped my tears and kissed him before hugging him again. I didn't want to let go, but when I heard a knock on the door, I knew it was time. I kissed his lips again, savoring their sweet nectar, then started toward the door, my hand sliding down his arms, breaking free when we were out of reach from one another.

When I opened the door and saw Bodya's colleague with two protectors, I turned back to my husband. "I still don't understand why you can't be the one who takes my memories away?"

"I told you already. He's not taking them away. He will just take a copy and save it on the glass memories." He brushed his fingers on my cheek. "Don't worry. Zil was working with me on the project, and I have already mapped out your mind for him."

I sighed. "Will I still remember you at the director's office tomorrow?"

Bodya turned to Zil, who nodded before my husband returned his gaze to me. "You will have to erase most of your memories today, but he will leave you enough so you can remember me until you erase the last sequence from your mind."

"I love you, Bodya. No matter what happens, don't you ever forget."

"I love you too," he said before quickly wiping away a tear.

With Bodya's last words, the memory slowly faded away. This time, however, everything became black again with Bodya and me at the center, our eyes meeting as if there was no one in the world but the two of us, yet he wasn't safe from the fading paint, even if it left him till the end. Then, like everything else, Bodya vanished into the darkness.

I opened my eyes, screaming and sobbing at the same time. My six seeds blinked out of order as my voice became louder and louder. Matso was right. When my memories became complete, and Bodya's face returned to them, my emotions found their true home.

I jumped up and paced the room, ignoring the broken glass on the ground and the cuts to my feet. The more I thought of Matso and Bodya, the louder I screamed. But when I realized how old my daughter would be, I began destroying every stick of furniture in the house piece by piece until I saw my reflection. Standing opposite the mirror, I tilted my head and inspected my red seed and the speed at which it blinked. I thought about removing it to dim my emotions.

"No," I said to myself, shaking my head. If I took the seed off my body, I would lose the pain, but also my anger at Matso. I had to feel it. I needed to embrace the hatred so I could find the old me again, the real Orantine who at that moment swore to kill Matso.

Looking back at the mirror, I noticed the white suit I wore to fit in Delphia. Disgusted by how I looked, I brushed my purple seed and the fabric transformed to liquid, changed its shape, and solidified again into a blue leather suit.

With my old uniform back on my body, I knew I was ready to hunt that Delphian down and bring him to his knees. But first, I had to save my daughter.

172

THE SINS THAT HAUNT US

"And this is my story." I sighed, lifting my eyes to look at the investigator. It didn't feel good to relive all the memories of my last seventeen years, and I cried again, but if there was one thing I had learned during this time, it was there's no fooling the Delphians.

"Alright, Miss Orantine. I would like to thank you for your honesty. Since you're short on time, I will go directly to my sentence." He adjusted the stack of papers in front of him in a perfect pile. "Here is how it works. I will give or deduct points for your most notable actions. You need to score ten or higher in order to be able to leave. If you gather less than ten but more than zero, your request will be denied, but no further actions will be taken against you. If you score less than zero, we will arrest you, and you will face an official judge to decide between life in prison or execution. Is that clear?"

I widened my eyes. "Why should there be a punishment at all? I came here willingly, and I told you everything with complete honesty."

"Just because it was your choice to come here doesn't mean we have to automatically forgive you. This is a society, and every action has a consequence, regardless of how you felt afterward."

"Fine." I exhaled loudly.

"I shall begin then." He retrieved a pencil from his pocket and started marking preprinted boxes on the paper atop the stack.

I glanced at it to see what it said and noticed that my life was broken into bullet points. I didn't need to tell him the story at all. *He knew everything and had prepared the file before he came here. That was such a waste of time.*

He raised his head to look at me. "Based on your story, I can conclude that you came to our faction with ill intentions. For that, I will deduct two points."

"What?" I raised my brows and crossed my arms in front of my chest. "I didn't do anything."

He put his pencil down. "I would appreciate it if you left your comments until I finished, Miss Orantine. I said nothing during your story. Now it is your turn to listen. Fighting my decisions will only deduct more points from you."

"This is stupid." I shook my head.

"And so is your insulting behavior."

I put my hand on my mouth and lowered my head.

"For your outburst, I will deduct another point."

My eyes widened and I clenched my fist, but I said nothing.

"For manipulating our asylum system and profiting from it when you had no right, I will deduct two points."

I clenched my teeth so hard it felt as though they were going to break.

"For abiding by the law for the last seventeen years and fulfilling all your civil service duties, I will award you six points."

I took a deep breath, thinking that things were turning. I started to calm down, but I still needed nine more points.

"For giving up on your faction and choosing us, I will give you seven points."

I felt my pulse begin to regulate.

"For marrying a Delphian, I will deduct four points."

I opened my mouth to speak, but he preceded me.

"I know that your marriage didn't break any rules, but it contradicted the Illicitums' guideline." He pulled a paper from the stack in front of him and handed it to me while saying what was on it, "Article Thirteen of the Forbidden Code is about cross-faction marriages. It states the following. 'While it isn't prohibited for two members from different factions to unite themselves with the bond of marriage, the parties in question forfeit their right of citizenship under all banners for the duration of their marriage. By signing the bond, they leave themselves exposed to whatever society deems a correct response at that time. All punishments are applicable except executions, which becomes definitive if the bond results in childbirth.'"

The investigator pulled the paper back. "You see, Miss Orantine, what we deemed correct was four points."

I sighed and lowered my head. I could see what he was trying to say. If I hadn't followed protocol when I married Matso, they would have killed and buried me like they did his parents, but they let it slide because we had no children together. I brought my head up and glanced at his paper. I could see he only had one item left to grade me on, but it was so far down on the list that I couldn't read it.

The investigator brought his eyes back to the paper. "For being manipulated by our faction, in which your decision to come here did not originate from you but resulted from the direct interference of a Delphian who changed the course of the future to bring you here, I give you six points."

"Yes," I shouted with a smile as I clapped my hands together.

"I appreciate your excitement, but I'm not finished yet."

I drew my brows together. There were no more boxes to check on his paper. I felt my heart race again, but this time, it was more fear than wonder.

"For applying to end your asylum, I will deduct one point."

I wanted to shout at him, but I knew it would cost me more points, so I redirected all my anger to my clenched fists until I felt my nails sink into my skin.

I spoke quietly, feeling a burn in my chest. "The application is an official procedure that your faction put in place. Don't you think it's strange that I lose a point for it?"

"No, Miss Orantine, I don't think so at all, especially since it says on the application that it would cost you one point.

"I feel—" I pressed my lips together and tensed the muscles in my face to keep my voice calm. "I feel that it's not fair. I already had ten points."

"As I told you, Miss Orantine, every action has consequences. If you didn't insult me when I started giving you the points, you would have had enough. He started signing the paper. "Your total is now nine points. There will be no further actions, but your application is denied.

He pulled a stamp out of his pocket, but before he united it with the paper, a small circle of red light appeared on his side of the table. He clicked it with his finger a couple of times before leaving his chair.

"I will be back, Miss Orantine. Please don't move." He left the room.

As I waited for him, I thought about my next course of action. There was no way I was going to let my daughter suffer. Tears ran down my cheeks as I remembered that I didn't even know what she looked like. At that moment, I made my decision. It didn't matter what they did to me later or if I had to live the rest of my life on the run. I was going to save Evailen, but before I could formulate my plan, he returned to the room.

He took his seat. "Alright, Miss Orantine, there has been a development in your story. I just found out that Matso was supposed to keep you in Delphia for three years. After that, he received orders to either manipulate your return or complete your circle of memories, so you could make your choice on your own. It turns out he declared that you had all your memories reinstated, and you chose to stay in Delphia. Since your story proves to me that this wasn't the case and you had no idea until yesterday, I will grant you six points."

He pulled a different stamp out of his pocket. "Your request is approved. You may go back to Lunar, and as an apology, I will waive the no-return rule. You may return to your house whenever you want."

The moment he said I could go, I ran out of the building. When I reached the roof exit, I pulled out my lotus pod and moved toward Lunar at top speed. It was time to show whoever ran Lantrix that my daughter wasn't someone they wanted to mess with.

LANTRIX

While sitting at the heart of my lotus pod and launching toward Lunar at top speed, I accessed the public records through my blue seed to learn everything about the owner of Lantrix.

Naytin Onak, sixty-two years old, married with three children. Decorated as the most successful Lunardis in the last three decades. He cofounded Lantrix with his childhood friend Dokan Azurin at the age of nineteen as a video game company. Within four years of its creation, the two men joined Lunar's top fifty richest men, but Azurin died shortly after that in a mysterious accident, leaving his partner Onak as the sole owner of a fast-growing enterprise. Naytin lives in a mansion near the southern borders of Lunar One.

Once I learned everything about him, I scanned the network for anything and everything that showed his face until I recognized every angle of it with and without light.

When I arrived at Lunar one, the capital of my faction, it was already dark. Yet, I felt strange. I barely recognized my own faction, but I didn't focus on that feeling. Instead, I thought about Naytin's mansion, and my pod followed the directions of my thoughts.

When I saw the grand house in the distance, I landed, retrieved my pod into my body, and hid close to the main gate. The house had several guards circling its front fence, and I watched their every movement while plotting my attack. There were nineteen by the front gate and around the extended metal barrier, plus six watchtowers, each loaded with an automatic machine gun.

Closing my eyes, I pressed both my blue and purple seeds simultaneously, activating heightened sight by forcing my brain to redirect ninety-nine-point-nine percent of its power into my sight while focusing the last point-one percent on the two fingers poised by my seeds. This ability enhanced my eyesight to a supernatural level. It allowed me to zoom in on the target and use night vision to better analyze everything. However, I had only fifty seconds to use it.

Since my brain focused only on my eyes, it couldn't send signals to any other part of my body, including my heart. Without the brain signals, the heart would stop pumping blood into my veins. But, since it took a full minute for the blood to circulate my body, If I was to brush my seeds again before the time was up, I would be able to restart my heart. That was why my fingers needed to be poised and ready for an instant move.

After scanning the weapons and the guards, I realized it was going to be easier than I thought. The guards used standard energy weapons, and since we designed our energy weapons specifically so they didn't work against our armor, I was sure I could take them on. After all, I was a member of the protector force before I became a spy, and we had advanced weapons that could subdue the masses if we needed to.

I brushed my black seed, releasing my armor from below my skin, enveloping my entire body in blue flexible voradium metal. Once the armor fully activated, my weapons also crawled forth, coming together the same way my clothes did.

Every Lunardis had one weapon attached to their armor. The weapons were always some sort of a gun but differed from one person to another as they took the shape of what the seed owner could think of on their thirteenth birthday. This is when Lunardis received an injection that embedded voradium metal into their bodies, creating our armor and weapon while connecting them to our black seed. I, however, had six. My regular weapon above my right wrist, two on my thighs, which the protector academy injected into my black seed and three on my belt that the agency added later.

I pulled out my left thigh gun, a long barrel revolver that diffused the chemicals in my blood and transformed them into tranquilizer bullets.

The next part of my plan didn't need a lot of work. I stepped out of my hiding spot and walked toward the guards, shooting at them one after the other before they could even realize they were under attack. Guards who didn't carry gear like mine were clearly no more than a fear factor, and I doubted they were even trained.

The bullets put them into an instant deep sleep, and those who managed to fire before I shot them dealt no damage against my armor. I walked through the gates, the garden, and into the mansion, dropping guards left and right. I was skilled with my guns and faster than the agency's best fighters. And though it was clear to me that I was extremely rusty, and my speed didn't match what I had once reached, I was still a lot better than them, and with the help of the muscle memories stored in my seeds, I was quickly reclaiming my skill.

When I infiltrated the residence, I walked up the stairs entering the main hall and stormed the rooms one by one until I found him. Naytin was sitting behind a desk, wearing sunglasses and a red bathrobe.

The moment I walked inside, I understood why he wore the glasses. Everything inside the room was pure gold, from the pen that matched the desk below it to the walls and the dozen statues of half-animal bodies. The source of light was a small golden lamp atop the desk, but its light reflected on every surface, multiplying its power until the entire room was as clear as day.

"Miss Orantine. Welcome," he said in a quiet voice as if he had been expecting me. "Please sit."

I narrowed my eyes. "If you think you can stall until the protectors get here, you're wrong. I can kill you faster than you can blink."

"I know." He smiled. "I'm well aware of your capabilities."

His calmness forced my heart to race and my thoughts to scramble. It took me nine minutes to get from the gate to his office. If he had seen through a security system, then he had enough time to raid our faction's network for my public record, but his tone suggested he knew I was a spy, which my faction would never announce even after my departure.

No, he knows more than that.

"Please sit," he said again. "I promise you, I'm only interested in a conversation, and there are no protectors coming."

His words appeared genuine despite my ill feelings about him. Still, I did as he suggested. "Do you know why I'm here?" I asked.

"You want me to spare your daughter." He picked up a golden pipe from his desk and started adding tobacco to it.

My eyes nearly widened, but I kept them neutral. We don't have tobacco in Lunar. Kala is the only faction that plants it, and they don't trade it with anyone. *How connected is this guy?*

"Are you going to spare her?" I pulled out one of my belt guns and pointed it at the space between his eyes. The gun was so small that I could hide it with both my hands but powerful enough to vaporize his entire head.

"I don't want to get rid of Evailen, she is one of the best programmers I've ever seen, and I wish she could continue working for me, but she wandered where she shouldn't have, and now she insists on transferring what she knows to the public." He lit his pipe and pulled a few puffs. "I even offered her a handsome reward in return for erasing that one memory, but she refused."

He breathed in another puff, appearing uninterested by the gun pointed at his head. "You see, I'm a businessman, and I didn't get where I am by playing nice. I have to protect my interests."

I gathered all my power into my voice. "Right now, it's in your best interest to keep her alive. Otherwise, I will introduce your head to my gun."

He chuckled. "You see, Miss Orantine, when you have done what I do for a living and for as long as I have, you realize that death, like everything in life, is a concept, and concepts can be altered." He exhaled a cloud of smoke. "If by death, you mean that my body will be no longer here, then I agree, but if you think that I will cease to exist, then you are wrong."

I didn't understand anything he spoke of, but it was clear that I didn't scare him, and that was how I knew he was willing to bargain.

I put a half-smile on my face. "If you don't care about what I could do to you, then why are we talking?"

"You are a smart woman." He tilted his head, eyeing me. "And a skilled one. Perhaps one of the best."

That, of course, wasn't true. I was indeed skilled, but I hadn't used any of my abilities for nearly two decades, during which I was bested by a Delphian. However, I couldn't show him my doubts, so I kept my features focused. "What do you want in return for my daughter's life?"

"Well, now that we can talk, do you mind putting that gun away?"

"I do." I bared my teeth. "The gun stays."

"Fine." He picked up his lighter and started to light his tobacco again. "In return for your daughter's life, you need to do a mission for me. Only one mission." He smiled. "Fair, isn't it?"

"What is the mission?"

"It's something you will like, actually. I want you to kill your husband, the Delphian one, not the other."

"What's in it for you?"

He looked into my eyes but said nothing, exhaling a cloud of smoke instead.

"You have to tell me if you want me to do it."

"We both know that you will accept the mission for your daughter's sake." He sighed. "I don't have to tell you anything, but I will because I wish to." He took another puff. "Prior to being criminalized for lying about manipulating you, your husband—"

"Don't call him that."

"The Delphian was investigating a few members of his faction that secretly work for me, and he plans to turn them in to the Skeptics in exchange for a pardon. I would rather not have my men exposed."

"Is this why my investigator waived the ban over my return to Delphia? Does he work for you too?"

Naytin took a long puff of his pipe while looking at me with a smirk but said nothing.

"Fine. If I do this, will you leave my daughter alone?"

"I can't exactly do that."

I stood and leaned forward, uniting the tip of my gun with his forehead.

"Relax," he said. "I won't kill her, but I still need to protect my interests. Tomorrow, the Protectors will choose Lunar's next Illicitum candidate. My saiters told me that if she were to join the Forbidden Palace, she would forget about her feud with us."

"My daughter would be an Illicitum?"

"You see how fair I am? You kill the man who took away your time with your true family, she gets the life everyone wishes for, and I continue living in peace without having to kill a smart, young woman. Everybody wins."

I nodded as I put my gun back in its holster. "I will do it, but only after they nominate her, and she actually goes."

"Agreed."

I took a few steps toward the door before turning back toward him. "Just know this. If anything happens to her—"

"You will kill me," he finished for me. "Don't worry, Miss Orantine, I'm a man of my word."

THE PEOPLE WE LOVE

When I left the mansion, I used my pod to go to my old apartment. The building where I used to once live looked different, taller and with modern walls. After inspecting the public records, I learned that neither Bodya nor my daughter lived there, but their new address was listed, and so I rushed to my new destination.

When I got there and saw their new home, my body froze, and I remained inside my pod, hovering slightly above a two-story house with a flat roof and mono-colored exterior. *A simple home for a simple man*. It was well past the middle of the night, and even though I had no intention of knocking on the door at this hour, I still couldn't bring my pod down. Instead, I continued to watch over the house through the entire night.

Shortly after the sun shed its light upon the world, I heard a scream and rushed my pod down to the side of the house, my gaze penetrating the window where the sound came from. At first, I saw nothing but a moving shadow, so I moved my pod to the side, and at that moment, I saw Bodya walk into the room. My red seed started blinking. He looked the same but also different. His face was as charming as I remembered, and reaching his late thirties seemed to bring the best out of his physic.

He was talking to someone I couldn't see, but I presumed it was Evailen. I moved my pod again, following the direction of Bodya's gaze until I managed to confirm my expectation. Evailen stood by a bed with a fist on her chest. She looked calm, unlike me, as I started shaking at the sight of her. For a moment, I felt cold, a feeling I rarely had, and this time I didn't touch my seeds to regulate my body's temperature. My attention was only with her.

Evailen was, of course, beautiful, more beautiful than I could have ever imagined. She was twenty, only two years younger than I was when I left the faction, but her face... I loved her face. Every detail in it reminded me of Bodya and myself at the same time. She looked innocent and fierce, calm and deadly. She had determination in her eyes that reminded me of my passion for new missions when I was younger.

A few tears strolled down my cheeks, but I quickly wiped them away before I used my seeds to heighten my hearing, focusing on their conversation.

"It's okay, sweetheart," Bodya said. "Just tell me what's bothering you, and I will make it go away."

Evailen sighed. "I just received a message from the leadership. They said the Illicitums have summoned me."

"Did they tell you why?" Bodya asked.

"No, they didn't, and it scares me."

"Don't worry, my dear. It will be okay."

"Do you really think so?"

"I do. The Illicitums may be the rulers of our world, but they are also just. I wouldn't worry about their summoning."

"I hope you are correct, Father." A moment of silence followed then Evailen spoke again. "Oh, Mighty Lotus, I'm late. I must leave now. I'm supposed to meet Cilia for breakfast."

When I saw Evailen leave the house, I contemplated following her, but I was less worried than before. If the Illicitums called for her, then Naytin was keeping his promise. A man who found his way to Kalanian tobacco and had Delphian saiters in his pocket wouldn't find it hard to influence the leaders of his own faction, and there was no playing with the Illicitums. If they summoned her, then it must have been because of Lunar's nomination.

Yet, I still followed her with my eyes when she left the house. I wanted to see her use her seed and pull out her pod, but she didn't. Instead, she walked. When she disappeared from my line of sight, I threw my gaze back to the house. My heart was still racing, and my seed continued to blink, but now that Bodya was alone, I thought it would be easier to go talk to him. At least, I hoped it would be easier, but my descent was slow, each step gained requiring more courage than the one before.

When my feet were finally on the ground, and my pod was back in my body, I moved toward the door. My progression, however, remained slow, slower even than before, but the distance was shorter, so it didn't take as long. My knock was also shy, missing my regular confidence, but maybe I had hoped Bodya wouldn't answer so I could walk away convinced that I tried. I wasn't even sure I wanted him to see me, but I couldn't run away from my truth. If I did, I would know for a fact that I was no longer Orantine Maray, and I would be unworthy of my seeds.

When Bodya opened the door, I had my gaze pointing at the ground. At that moment, I realized I hadn't reversed my enhanced hearing and was able to hear his heartbeat. The rhythm of his beats seemed to be as uneven as mine, perhaps even faster. Had I raised my gaze and looked at his face, I would have been able to understand the meaning of his elevated heartbeats, but I couldn't. I didn't dare look into his eyes.

"You are back," he said.

My eyes remained focused on my feet, but I felt a smile in his voice, though faint and possibly a leap from my imagination. I nodded in silence, moving no other muscle. I wanted to run into his arms and beg for his forgiveness. I wanted to apologize for the years I stole away from us, for blocking all his calls, and for leaving him alone to raise our daughter. Tears fell down my cheeks and landed on the floor. He could see them, I was sure.

"Would you like a drink?" he asked, and before I gave him an answer, he walked back into the house, leaving the door wide open.

I followed his steps into the kitchen, glancing at the house without fully raising my head. It was nice, cozy, and well organized, as he always was.

He took two glasses from a high cupboard and placed them on the kitchen table between us before pouring some tomato juice into them. *He still remembers it's my favorite.*

"I see you didn't lose your beauty." He pushed my glass toward me.

"Thank you." I nodded.

"How are you?"

"Angry and disoriented."

He paused for a second and sipped a little from his glass before leaning forward to meet my lowered gaze. Knowing that there was no avoiding it any longer, I raised my head and looked back into his eyes, and my tears exploded again. I tried to control my emotions, but for the first time, I failed. He didn't say anything, though, and waited until I dried my tears.

"Was it you?" Bodya asked.

"What?"

"Did you get the leadership to send her to the Forbidden Palace?"

"Something like that."

"I knew you would fix it." His grin widened. "She is going to be an Illicitum, isn't she?"

"Yes, but I assume she will have to go through trials first or something. I heard these things have qualifying rounds."

"I'm not worried about that. Your daughter is fierce." He paused. "Just like you," he added.

"I wouldn't wish that upon her."

"Then you don't know your true worth."

"Stop it," I said in a hushed voice.

"What? I'm only speaking the truth."

"You're talking as if I was here yesterday and every day for the last seventeen years. You're treating me as if I never left."

"You are here now." He clasped his hands together and placed them on the table. "How did you think I was going to react?"

"I don't know. Be angry, hate me. You could even kick me out."

"We're not kids anymore to let our emotions get the better of us."

"But you must feel these emotions. You can't possibly be okay with all of this." I raised my tone of voice without realizing it.

186

"Okay? With my wife being with another man? Listening to him instead of reason? With you being away for all that long? With lying to my daughter every day about where her mother was so she wouldn't feel abandoned?" He shook his head. "I was never okay with this, and I don't think I will ever be. But I had years to deal with it and prepare for this moment."

"You knew I was coming back?"

"I hoped you would. I fought for your return until Delphia contacted our leadership to force me to stay away from their faction. I woke up every day wishing it would be the day, and today it finally is." His face reclaimed his smile. "What happened is in the past, and I believe the damage is bigger on you."

He sighed. "I don't know how I would feel if I woke up one day and realized I missed out on Evailen growing up." He paused. "That was mean, and I'm sorry."

"No, it wasn't." I wiped away my new stream of tears. "It does hurt, a lot, but your suffering was—"

"Stop this," he interrupted. "We don't need to argue over who suffered more. It's not a competition. We both messed up one way or another."

I shook my head. "It's just—"

"This is life," he interrupted again. "There's no changing what happened, and it will do us nothing to dwell on the past. What matters is you're here now, and it's time to think about the future."

"I'm not sure my future will be that bright."

"Why not?" Bodya drew his brows together.

"I'm sure the agency is looking for me now, and once they catch me, they will sentence me to death or worse."

"No one is looking for you. They were angry at first, but not when they learned the truth. Fourteen years ago, we received a message from Delphia explaining what they did and gave our faction more access to theirs in an attempt for reconciliation. They also said you knew the truth and chose to remain there. Your director said he wasn't surprised. He believed you were ashamed of yourself and were afraid to return, but I never believed that you knew. Especially because I tried many times to reach you and through many ways, but Matso always found a way to counter back and ban me from contacting you. This is why I was certain that if you *did* know, you would come back. At least for Evailen."

"I would have, I swear." I jumped on his words.

"I know." He smiled. "Breakfast?"

I shook my head and he prepared himself something to eat. When he returned to the table, he gazed at me with a wide smile.

"So?" He took a bite from his sandwich. "Do you need a place to stay?"

My eyes widened as I raised my brows. "Do you want me back?"

"If you want to."

"How can you be so cool about this?"

"I told you, I had a lot of time to deal with my anger. Does it hurt? Yes, but it also hurt because you weren't here. I'm a scientist, and my job is to find the best outcome for failed scenarios." He sighed. "In the end, I realized I would always love you, and I liked life better when you were in it. I have another chance at being with you. Why should I waste it?"

"I take it there's no one else?"

He chuckled. "There never was."

I narrowed my eyes and playfully looked into his.

"They were only flings, I promise."

"I believe you." My grin finally found its way back to my face.

"I take that as you will consider it?" he asked, referring to my smile.

I lowered my chin and shook my head. "I don't think it will work out."

"Why not?" he asked with a pitched tone.

"He broke me. That arrogant Delphian stole my life, and I don't think I can ever recover from that. It wouldn't be fair to you."

"Let me be the judge of what's fair or not fair when it comes to me. Don't use me as an excuse."

"I just don't think it will work. I have too much baggage now, and I need to deal with it on my own." I stood. "I need to go before Evailen returns."

"You don't want to meet her?"

"Of course I do, but now is not the right time. I'm not ready yet."

Bodya walked me to the door. "What did you give up?" he asked. "For her safety."

"I promised to do a mission."

"Is it dangerous?"

I looked at him with tender eyes before I moved closer and whispered in his ear. "You're the best Bodya, and I'm truly sorry." I printed a long kiss on his cheek and moved out of the house with hurried steps.

He followed me through the garden and grasped my arm. "After you finish your mission and have had enough time to think about it, how about a date?"

I turned my head back, revealing my wide grin to him. "Maybe."

EPILOGUE
ILLICITUM: NEXT GENERATION

Evailen joined her friend Cilia in Café Six, which topped one of Lunar's highest buildings. She sat at a round table with a glass top that matched a dozen more scattered around her. Next to her, a glass railing overlooked Lunar's nine high towers, each in a different color. Smaller buildings with twelve stories or less spread between the towers, each displaying some form of advertisement banners that at times took over an entire building. Hundreds of Lotus pods buzzed around the city, and even though they followed predestined routes, there was a sense of chaos in the way they moved.

Evailen enveloped her pale body with a black tank top and a skin-tight trouser, leaving her six seeds visible, their glow slightly dimmed by the sun. Her gaze darted around, ignoring meeting her friend's eyes.

"So?" Cilia asked, her thick figure filling her small metal chair. "Are you still planning to move forward with what you told me?"

Evailen didn't answer. Instead, she called a waitress and asked for a pen, still avoiding her friend. When she got her pen, Evailen pulled a napkin from the center of the table and wrote four words on it. "The Illicitums summoned me." Placing her pen on the table, she pushed the tissue toward Cilia, who grabbed it quickly with concern in her eyes.

Cilia's eyes widened, but she also looked relieved. "You could have just told me. There was no need for all of that."

"I know," Evailen said with a smile. "But it was fun to act as if it was something dangerous."

"It still could be," Cilia quickly countered, though she rolled her eyes at her friend's behavior.

Evailen sighed and straightened. "I agree, but my father said I shouldn't worry."

"Do you think it's about what you found at Lantrix?"

"I don't know. I keep telling myself that there's no other reason, but since when did the Illicitums interfere in inner faction matters?"

"True." Cilia scratched her chin and leaned back. "It does make me wonder, but my main worry is you. I'm afraid that if you keep insisting on exposing Lantrix, something bad will happen."

"What are they going to do? Kill me?"

Cilia said nothing, but Evailen could see that she wanted to say yes to her sarcastic question. It was written all over her face. "Relax, Cilia. Even though I'm sure they will continue trying to silence me, I don't think it will ever come to that."

Cilia shrugged. "Tell me, what was it you uncovered again?"

Evailen sighed and spoke in a quieter voice. "They are stealing the green seeds of the recently dead."

"Exactly, and what makes you think that people who are dabbling in Lunardis souls are above killing?"

"It's not the same. The act is unethical, disgusting, and outrageous, but the people I saw were already dead. Surely, they won't be killing their own people."

"Evailen, my dear, sometimes I see in you the smartest person in our faction, but then you say something like this, and all I can think about is how naïve you are. Lantrix is the largest corporation in Lunar. It would be foolish to think that what you discovered is their only dirty secret. In our world, companies run the scene, and the bigger they are, the more dangerous they become."

"Does this apply to your father's company too? Vtec is among the top players," Evailen said with a sarcastic tone.

"Yes," Cilia answered with a firm voice, her expression serious. "My father abandoned his youngest just because she could have tarnished his reputation and is forcing his eldest to marry his rival for a bigger share of the market. I can't even imagine what he would do to those who are not of his blood."

"I'm sorry, Cilia. I didn't mean to be insensitive."

"I don't want your apology, and we are not here to worry about my situation. Limited as it may be, I know how to navigate my life. It's you I'm concerned about. You need to grow up, Evailen and deal with the world the way it is. This ideology you insist on embracing will cost you your life and take away my best friend."

"Then I must apologize again. This is who I am, Cilia, and you have always known me as a woman of truth. I will make it my mission to expose Lantrix, and if they truly want to kill me as you say, then let them come."

"Fine, Evailen. I know there's no changing your mind when you put it to something, but at least let me handle the situation. Perhaps, this way, I can guarantee you will make it out in one piece."

Evailen laughed.

"What?" Cilia asked.

"This is so you. You always pull me to the worst-case scenario, so I agree to play by your rules. You present it as a compromise, but we both know the truth. This is what you wanted all along."

"That's not true."

Evailen ignored her words and continued. "At first, you convinced me to wait for a week before I took any action and now that the time is up, you don't want me to move forward without you approving my next step."

"I told you—"

"Yeah, yeah," Evailen interrupted while rising to her feet. "I won't win with you either, so here's my compromise. You have until I come back from the Forbidden Palace to present your plan. If I like it, I will follow it. Otherwise, I will do what I see best." She pushed her chair closer to the table.

"Where are you going?" Cilia asked. "We didn't even have breakfast yet."

"I have a summoning to answer. One doesn't keep the Illicitums waiting."

"Surely you can eat first. It's not like they are going to make you one of them."

Both girls laughed at the concept and how impossible it sounded. There could be no more than four Illicitums in the world of Mastoperia, and a new generation came only once every two and half centuries. And even though it was time for a new ascension, each faction could only nominate one person. The four candidates would then compete for who would become their leader and the Umholi of the entire continent. Therefore, factions nominated their most elite warrior. They thought that if their candidate was to sit on the throne, they too would have the upper hand. It never worked like that, yet they continued trying.

Still laughing, Evailen left. One didn't keep the Illicitums waiting indeed. Her mind didn't even entertain the idea of ever becoming an Illicitum. Surely this was not why they summoned her. Surely, she was not her faction's candidate. How could she be? Evailen was no more than a videogame programmer, a position carried by many of her people.

Evailen released her pod and rode it, thinking of the Forbidden Palace as her destination.

If only she knew her mother's bargain, perhaps she would have had an idea of the future that awaited her.

AFTER WORD

Thank you for reading my work. Your support means a lot. It helps me continue doing what I truly love, writing the stories I want to tell. At the end of Twelve Jackals, and in this very section, I wrote a short story from my childhood and spoke about how that one event could explain my love for fantasy and storytelling. I would like to do the same here, but this time I will tell you of the fantasy in my life.

The story you are about to read is one hundred percent true. I will only change the name of the second character for the sake of their privacy.

Road Trip

Moud tightened his grip on the wheel and continued to focus on the road. He drove on a single-lane, two-way highway with no barrier in the center. For that, he stayed true to the speed limit. He worried, especially after residential houses and busy sidewalks replaced the vast farms that had accompanied him for the last five hours.

"Did you see that?" Mira took her feet off the dashboard and pushed her head out the window. "There are at least ten donkeys walking about with no riders."

"They're probably going home," Moud said, keeping his eyes forward.

Mira pulled her head back inside. "You don't find that strange?"

"We're on a road trip to the south of Egypt, Mira. Here, this view is completely normal."

"Sure, sure." Mira took out her camera and began filming the scenery. "I need to keep an eye out."

Moud smiled. Three years ago, Mira left France and came to live in Egypt. Yet, this was her first trip to Luxor, the city of ancient monuments. Therefore, he couldn't blame her for being excited. After all, the south was a world of its own, one that was completely different from that of Cairo.

He continued to drive, and soon, civilization disappeared again, allowing Moud to take a breather, for while the road remained narrow, it was now bordered by sand dunes on one side and a canal on the other.

When he found himself stuck behind a motorcycle, he slowed all the way to twenty kilometers per hour. *At this rate, it would take seven hours to reach their destination.* So, when he found an opening, Moud decided to take over the moto. He slipped to the left and pressed on the gas. Only the rider had different thoughts. Apparently, he noticed Mira and decided to smile at the foreigner to his side. He sped up to match the speed of the car.

At the sight of a vehicle coming from the opposite direction, Moud had to slow down. He needed to be back in the correct lane, but the motorcycle wouldn't let him. The rider decreased his speed again.

A sudden and unavoidable break forced the car into a semi-spin. Moud turned the wheel toward the dunes lest they crash into the water on the opposite side of the road. The car flipped onto its side, coming to a stop inches from the sand.

Moud and Mira were lucky they didn't get injured.

When they climbed out of the car from the driver's side, they found a large crowd of people gathered around. *Where did they come from?* Moud had no clue. There were two other cars on the road, he remembered, but this many people certainly couldn't have fit into just those two vehicles.

Together, with those good people, they managed to right the tilted car until it fell back on its wheels. Damage report: The right mirror and the bumper had fallen off, and the car lost its reverse option. The vehicle had an automatic gear system.

Now that all was back to normal, well, sort of, Moud and Mira choose to move forward. After a quick stop at the police station—yes, among the crowd there were two officers on a motorcycle who insisted on going there to make sure the foreigner was alright—where they pretended to be married to avoid further questioning. After a tight maneuver to bring the unreversible car back on the road, they continued their journey.

About an hour later, they came across a car shop. Moud asked them if they could put the bumper back in place quickly, to which the mechanic nodded.

Hood popped, and restoration ongoing, Moud lost sight of Mira, who remained inside the car while he surveyed the work. A few minutes later, two men in long tunics—a thobe—and a scarf wrapped around their heads approached Moud. A strap around their shoulders held their AK47 rifles to their sides.

"Are you the one who's been in an accident?" asked one of the two.

"What accident?"

"The one where the car flipped up the road."

"Umm...yeah."

Confusion popped in Moud's head. *How could they know about the event that fast?* But they seemed nice enough with their questions that he eased his concern.

A few minutes into the conversation, Moud went to retrieve something from inside the car, and...

Mira wasn't there.

He panicked, his gaze darting left and right, his feet unstable on the ground. *No, no.* They'd distracted him with a conversation, so he didn't notice when they kidnapped her.

"Where is she?" Moud demanded, his voice loud and his heart pounding in his chest.

"Where is who?"

They're pretending to be innocent. But what could he do?

Moud ran left and right to see where they could have taken her. Sweat began pouring from his body. He noticed a pharmacy a few meters away and sprinted there to see if the people inside might have seen something.

He flung the door open and rushed inside, his breath heaving and the possibilities of what the men could have done with her pinging around in his brain. He scanned the occupants of the pharmacy and...

Mira was sitting inside, drinking a glass of tea, and laughing with the pharmacist. Moud's heart stopped, but what could he say? It wasn't her fault he didn't see her get out of the car and walk away.

Moud and Mira continued their journey, the bumper and reverse gear now fixed but with no side mirror. He confessed his brief moments of fear to Mira, and they laughed together. Their journey was almost over. They would soon get to their hotel and rest.

They'd booked a place with an authentic experience. Something that should have been familiar to Moud, except it wasn't. He should have dug deeper into that slogan. In all fairness, the insides of the rooms did look as advertised. Only they weren't rooms, but huts in the backyard of a house where chicken and ducks roamed freely between the chambers and the cannabis plants that apparently were included in the price of the room and guests could use them at well. Luckily, they had a delicious meal waiting for them, which came accompanied by Bob Marley's "One Love," a song that would play in a loop over the following four days.

The End

Writing is a lot more than a passion to me, and while I enjoy the process of producing books, it's not without its struggles. So, if you like my artist side and would like to help me continue making books, you can do that by:

- Reading the next book in the series, Ascension Trials.
- Leaving an honest review, which would be greatly appreciated.
- Discovering my other series, Earth Guardians.

If you would like to know more about the universe I created, writing updates, or the occasional personal news, you can join my newsletter Through this link:

https://moudadel.com/newsletter/

If you want to chat directly with me about the world, you can find the series Facebook group through this link:

https://www.facebook.com/groups/329519658631787

Once again, thank you, and I hope to see you in the next story.

MOUD ADEL

CPSIA information can be obtained
at www.ICGtesting.com
Printed in the USA
LVHW090309010821
694233LV00013B/407/J